The Evil Emir of Transoxiana

Ray Filby

The Evil Emir of Transoxiana

Publisher : Midhurst

Published by Midhurst

This is a work of fiction.
Any resemblance to actual persons,
living or dead, is purely coincidental.

Midhurst.
2, Freers Mews,
Warwick,
Warwickshire,
CV34 6DP

ISBN 978-1-9160485-8-4

http://midhurstpublishing.uk

<u>Acknowledgements</u>

The author would like to thank his wife, Sue, both for proof reading and for her patience and encouragement during the writing of this story.

The cover picture is the Amir Timur Museum, Tashkent

Contents

Introduction

Becky meets with her special friends, Jason, Bill and Liz, to tell them she is being posted to Transoxiana. She needs to explain exactly where she will be working, that she will be accompanied by Jason and that she will be spending some time with her Kyrgyz penfriend, Askari, and her husband, Temier.

During Becky's stay with Askari, Temier falls foul of an extremist Islamic cleric, the self-styled, Emir of Transoxiana. The resourcefulness of Becky and Jason, helped by Bill and Liz who travel out to join them, is needed to keep Askari and Temier safe from the Evil Emir. In spite of the danger being faced, they all manage to have the experiences in Transoxiana which make their stay both exciting and enjoyable.

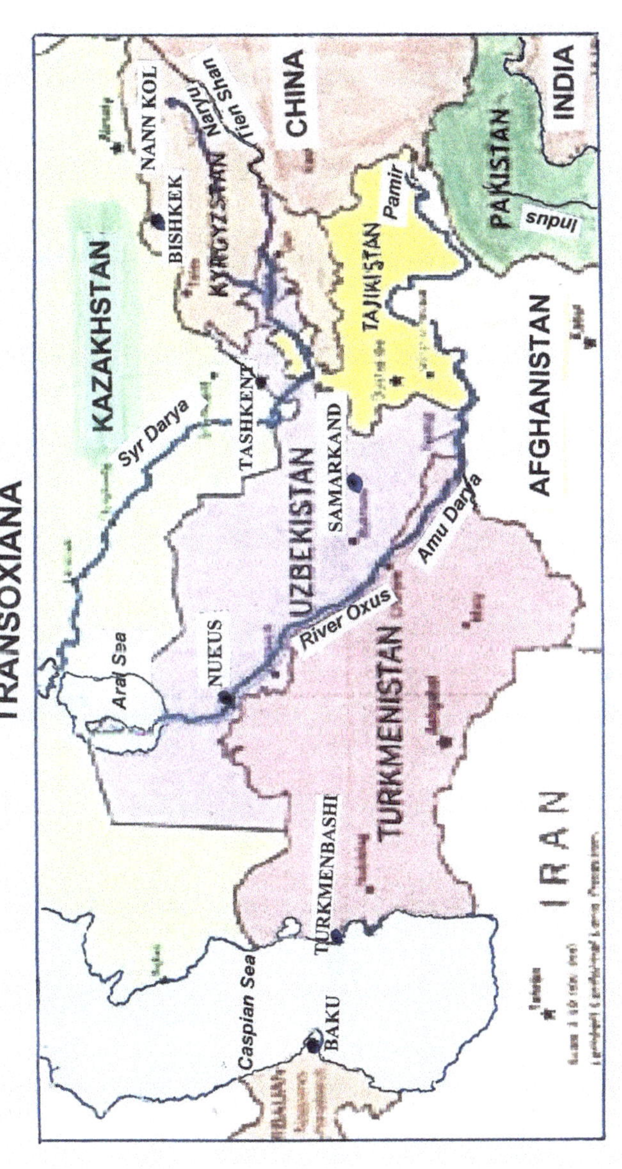

TRANSOXIANA
KAZAKHSTAN
KYRGYZSTAN
UZBEKISTAN
TAJIKISTAN
TURKMENISTAN
AFGHANISTAN
CHINA
INDIA
PAKISTAN
IRAN
NANN KOL
BISHKEK
Naryu
Tien Shan
Pamir
Indus
TASHKENT
SAMARKAND
NUKUS
TURKMENBASHI
BAKU
Syr Darya
Amu Darya
River Oxus
Aral Sea
Caspian Sea

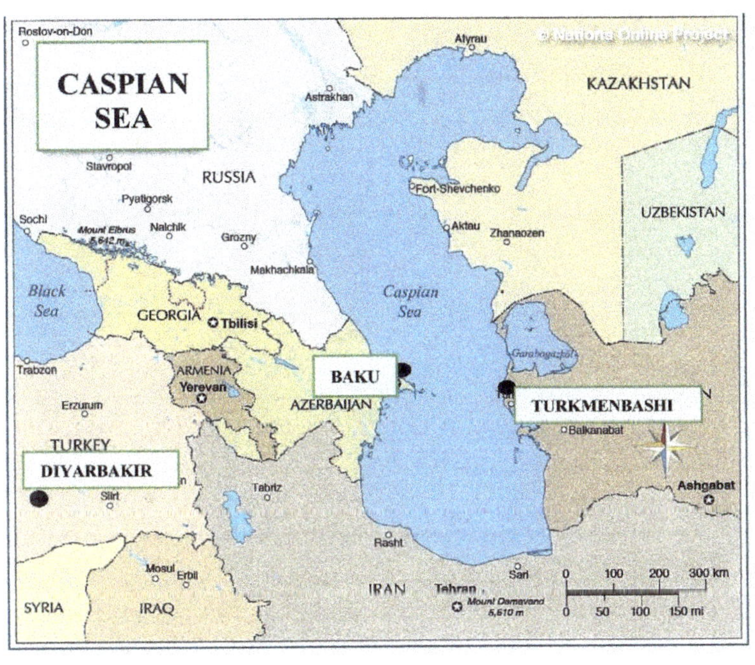

CASPIAN SEA
Rostov-on-Don
Atyrau
KAZAKHSTAN
Astrakhan
Stavropol
RUSSIA
Pyatigorsk
Fort-Shevchenko
Sochi
Mount Elbrus
5,642 m
Nalchik
Aktau
Zhanaozen
UZBEKISTAN
Grozny
Makhachkala
Black
Sea
Caspian
Sea
GEORGIA
Tbilisi
Garabogazkol
Trabzon
ARMENIA
BAKU
Yerevan
TURKMENBASHI
Erzurum
AZERBAIJAN
Balkanabat
TURKEY
DIYARBAKIR
Ashgabat
Siirt
Tabriz
Rasht
Mosul
Erbil
Sari
0   100   200   300 km
IRAN
Tehran
SYRIA
IRAQ
Mount Damavand
5,610 m
0   50   100   150 mi
© Nations Online Project

Chapter 1
Transoxiana

"I'm being posted to Transoxiana!"   declared the young woman.

The young woman was Becky Collins. She was a tall attractive blond. During the day she would be seen attired in a smart skirt suit. However, while relaxing at home, she wore a patterned jumper and black, loosely fitting trousers. Her hair was shoulder length and curled at the ends. Becky had recently completed a degree in modern languages at Oxford University and had secured a post with the diplomatic service. With a view to being able to offer something different on the job market, she had studied two Turkic languages, Kyrgyz and Uzbek. These were not available as mainstream languages at Oxford and she had spent six months at Indiana University in the United States where these languages were available in their Department of Central Eurasian Studies. Becky had a flare for languages and was already fluent in French, German and Russian. Her unusual choice of languages paid off. The Department of International Trade showed no hesitation in offering Becky a prestigious job. She had done well in the civil service exams she was required to take and she had rare language qualifications in an area where the Department wished to establish trading relationships. Post Brexit initiatives had already seen the signing of a trade deal with Turkey and an approach to join the Comprehensive and Progressive Agreement for Trans Pacific Partnership (CPTPP). Central Asia was an area which looked suitable for forging new trade relationships. They were a promising market for British goods and had significant deposits of valuable minerals including gold, uranium, antimony and rare earth metals which could be important in the development of high technology components.

Becky was meeting with her three special friends in her spacious study/bedroom. The bookshelves which lined the wall displayed a good mix of books, novels written in modern languages, computer manuals, classical novels, travel guides and Christian literature. An account has been given in an earlier novel of how Becky and her three friends had worked as a team with complementary technical skills to thwart the activities of an international gang of forgers. These forgers had holed up in the local castle in Easingdale which they had purchased from the aristocrat for whom it had been his ancestral residence. Uncovering the activities of this gang was a remarkable achievement in view of the fact that Becky and her friends were still at school at the time.

Becky had arranged for one of these special friends, Jason Markham, to accompany her on the trip she was about to undertake. Even with the diplomatic cover provided for her projected enterprise, it was considered unsafe for a young woman to travel alone in the unfamiliar territory to which Becky's mission would take her. Jason was of African-Caribbean origin. His grandparents had come to Britain on the Windrush in response to the invitation issued by the government to inhabitants of the West Indies to come to Britain to fill the many job vacancies which were emerging in post-war Britain. Jason was resourceful and showed great leadership qualities. Like Becky, he too had studied at Oxford, gaining his BA in Maths and Computer Science and going on for a further year to take a masters degree (MMathComSci). He was already aware of the location of Transoxiana and had done some research about the area when he had agreed to accompany Becky on this adventure. Becky's other two friends had been unaware of her plans and looked at each other with some degree of amazement. They hadn't heard of Transoxiana.

Where was it? Why was Becky going there? Bill Compton and Liz Holmes turned their amazed gazes back to Becky.

Bill was a tall, fair-haired young man with an athletic build. He was casually dressed in Levi jeans and a navy sweater. He wore leather trainers over his patterned socks. Bill was a graduate in Maths and Computer Science from Imperial College, London, where he had been awarded a BEng degree. One sensed that Bill had a great sense of humour.

Liz Holmes was a very personable brunette who wore her hair rather longer than Becky's. Even though casually dressed in a pale blue T-shirt and well-fitting black jeans, she conveyed the impression of being a very neat and smart person. She was well balanced with good inter-personal skills. Her reading extended well beyond the technical books which had supported her studies and she had a good knowledge of English literature and history. Geography was not her forte and she shared Bill's ignorance of the location of Transoxiana. Liz had studied in the Department of Computer Science and Technology at Cambridge University. She had graduated with a BA and had done a further year's study to obtain an MEng degree. She retained contact with 'The Ring', an organisation by which graduates in technology from Cambridge University kept in touch.

As you will have gathered, these four friends were all extremely bright young people. They had had no trouble in securing the A* grades they needed in their A levels to secure places in the prestigious universities they had attended.

Becky had anticipated that her friends would not be familiar with Transoxiana.

"Transoxiana isn't a country, it's a vast region of central Asia, around and to the east of the Oxus river."

Liz's face immediately lit up in recognition. The mention of the Oxus river triggered something in her memory.

"Of course, of course," she exclaimed. "How well I remember reading Matthew Arnold's epic poem, Sohrab and Rustum, in class at school. I learned great chunks of that piece of poetry by heart. Liz waxed lyrical as she started to quote parts of the poem.

And the first grey of morning fill'd the east,
And the fog rose out of the Oxus stream.
But all the Tartar camp along the stream
Was hushed and still, the men were plunged in
sleep;
Sohrab alone, he slept not; all night long
He had lain wakeful tossing on his bed;
But when the grey dawn stole into his tent,
He rose, and clad himself, and girt his sword,
And took his horseman's cloak, and left his tent,
And went abroad into the cold wet fog,
Through the dim camp to Peran-Wisa's tent.
Through the black Tartar tents he passed which
stood
Clustering like bee-hives on the low flat strand
Of Oxus, where the summer floods overflows
When the sun melts the snows in high Pamere.

Oh, I could quote so much more. I find the final
verse describing the Oxus rising from its source
particularly evocative.

In his high mountain cradle in Pamere,
A foil'd circuitous wanderer – till at last
The long'd for dash of waves is heard, and wide
His luminous home of waters opens, bright
And tranquil, from whose floor the new-bathed
stars

Emerge and shine upon the Aral Sea."

Becky closed her eyes as she emotionally completed this monologue. "Oh, how I wish I could stand on the shore of the Aral Sea and imagine the armies in battle array, waiting for the trumpet which would sound the charge and hear the clash of steel on steel as their cohorts met and brave men battled for supremacy over the land they had traversed."

Becky paused to realign her thoughts.

"However, that poem doesn't involve armies waging conflict but just a battle to the death between single champions selected from the opposing armies. A very pragmatic way of settling a battle, one that didn't involve two armies inflicting such damage on each other that even the victor would be weakened to the extent that it couldn't defend itself against attack from another army. The poem is a tragedy. Sohrab longed to meet his father, Rustum, whom he knew was a renowned soldier in the Persian army. The Persian champion who came out to face Sohrab was indeed Rustum, but he had disguised his identity and didn't even realise he had a son among the Tartars until Sohrab was mortally wounded. Then they each discovered the other's identity."

"That sounds my sort of poem," said Bill, "but I can't remember reading that poem in class at school and I was in the same form as you, Liz."

"That's because we read it during our options afternoon. I had opted for classical poetry and you had joined the robotics group," explained Liz.

There was a pause before Jason spoke.

"Sadly, the vision you wish for Liz, is no longer possible. As recently as 1989, the Aral Sea covered the full area it had occupied for centuries. When it came under Soviet control, various irrigation schemes were developed which involved diverting rivers and waterways which had replenished the Aral Sea since time immemorial. The sea has now shrunk to only ten percent of its former area! This has been a major, major ecological disaster. Half-hearted attempts to replenish the sea have failed. What's left of the sea is heavily polluted. An island in the sea used by the Soviets for testing biological weapons is poisoned with anthrax and the plague. As the sea dried, this contaminated island has become joined up with the land which had surrounded the sea, posing a threat to both human and animal life!"

The young people looked stunned and shocked.

"It's terrible what irresponsible governments around the world are doing to the environment," commented Bill. "When Trump was President of America, they seemed reluctant to take the measures every other nation had adopted to get the climate back under control and what's happening to the Amazon rainforests is absolutely criminal. Sadly, there seems to be nothing we can do about it."

Becky added,

"The Soviet Union has been the most recent imperial power to annexe these vast central Asian territories whose states became designated 'Soviet Republics'. In the past, a number of superpowers of their day had occupied these territories to create the then largest known empires of their time."

Liz seemed to be the most knowledgeable about the history of the area and explained,

"The poem, Sohrab and Rustum, is set in a period when the Persians and the Tartars competed for the territory. The lands were taken over by Alexander the Great when he defeated the Persians. In mediaeval times, a great Mongol Empire, which included Transoxiana, was created by Genghis Khan. Later, this land was conquered by another war lord, Tamburlaine. The Russians moved into these lands during the nineteenth century when Russia was ruled by the Czars. As we know, Czarist Russia gave place to the Soviet Union. The states which are included in the area we know as Transoxiana didn't become independent until 1990 after Glasnost when they separated from the Soviet Union."

"Thank goodness for Gorbachev," added Jason. "He at least was a politician with realistic vision."

The young people sat in silence for a while, musing on their recent conversation. Their thoughts on what might be regarded as a romantic period of history were calming and pleasant but their reflections on environmental issues were sad and disturbed.

"So then," interjected Bill, "Which part of Transoxiana are you being posted to, Becky?"

Chapter 2
Kyrgyzstan

"The country I'm going to first is called Kyrgyzstan, but I will also be spending time in Uzbekistan," replied Becky.

Bill and Liz again looked in puzzlement at each other. They'd heard of Uzbekistan but Kyrgyzstan was a new name for them.

"Kyrgyzstan is one of the smaller central Asian republics," continued Becky, realising that few people would be familiar with this name. "These central Asian republics are all 'stans', an ancient Persian name for 'country'. A large part of Kyrgyzstan is mountainous. The Tien Shan range, which may be regarded as the northern end of the Himalayan mountain range system, covers the south and east of the country."

"Will you be able to visit Everest while you're out there?" asked Bill.

"I don't think so," replied Becky. "but there'll be enough mountains where I'm going. Even though dwarfed by the majestic Himalayas, its tallest mountain, Jengish Chokusu, is the most northerly peak at over seven thousand metres tall which exceeds even the highest Alpine peaks. Indeed, Kyrgyzstan is often regarded as the Switzerland of Central Asia and as such, it has considerable potential as a tourist destination."

"How far will you be from the sea?" asked Liz.

"Kyrgyzstan is further from the sea than any other country but shares a border with China which of course has a coastline," answered Becky. "I'll also be spending time in Kyrgyzstan's neighbour, Uzbekistan which, unless you count tiny Liechtenstein sandwiched between Switzerland and Austria, is the only doubly landlocked country in the world. It is bordered by Kazakhstan, Tajikistan, Afghanistan, Turkmenistan and of course, Kyrgyzstan, all of which are landlocked."

They all wanted to know what the people living there were like.

"Kyrgyzstan is quite cosmopolitan," Becky explained. "The largest ethnic group are the Kyrgyz which make up three-quarters of the population but there are a very significant number of Russians. Indeed, the capital city, Bishkek, is principally occupied by Russians. Among other ethnic groups are Uzbeks, Dungans, Uyghurs, Tajiks, Kazakhs and Ukrainians. The state is officially bilingual with both Kyrgyz and Russian being spoken as first and second languages. Uzbek is also widely spoken and nearly thirty thousand people speak English as a second language."

"How extensive is Russian influence?" asked Bill.

Becky started to explain the political system in Kyrgyzstan.

"Around 1990, the country became independent of the Soviet Union but it took quite a long time to stabilise. It's now a parliamentary democracy with an elected government. However, in the early days of independence, there were riots and inter-ethnic violence between the Kyrgyz and the Uzbeks. Corruption was rife. Groups connected with organised crime competed for power and a number of newly elected members of parliament were assassinated. In 2010, there were serious clashes between the Kyrgyz and Uzbeks in Osh, the second largest city in the country, but the government managed to control these and bring about order, averting the threat of civil war. Since then, the country has settled into stability."

"Can it really be regarded as a true democracy?"

It was Jason who asked this time. He had researched the geography of the country but knew little about its politics.

"Yes. It has a genuinely free news media and an active political opposition which acts within the spirit of democracy. There is still more corruption than there should be and being a largely Muslim country, there are certain limitations on human rights as the gay rights activists face a degree of persecution. However, the country is advancing towards what we might regard as a liberal democratic society."

"We know that you'll be staying with your Christian penfriend. Will there be many other Christians out there?" enquired Liz.

"Eighty percent of the population would describe themselves as Muslim but for many, this represents a cultural background rather than an active faith. The majority of practicing Muslims are Sunni. Christianity is also practiced, the largest group being Russian Orthodox, but there are smaller numbers of Lutherans, Roman Catholics and

Baptists. Also, there are a significant number of Jehovah's Witnesses."

Jason, Liz and Bill listened intently to this concise summary of the country to which Becky was being posted but Liz and Bill still wondered just why she was going there. Becky continued.

"Since Brexit, this country has been seeking to find new markets and my employers, the Department of International Trade, are investigating the possibility of striking a trade deal with the Kyrgyz. The country looks like a promising market for our goods and has valuable mineral deposits including gold, uranium, antimony and rare earth metals which we would find very useful. It would appear that rare earth metals may be specially valuable in the development and manufacture of modern electronic components. I've been sent to undertake an initial investigation of the potential for establishing trading partnerships and to identify suitable contacts for further trade negotiations.

The Department have told me that it wouldn't be safe for a woman to travel alone in such a remote part of the world and have asked me to find someone who might be prepared to accompany me. Jason has kindly agreed to travel with me."

Bill and Liz were not entirely surprised to hear this. Becky and Jason had been able to maintain their close friendship during the time they were both at Oxford. Jason was known to be a very resourceful young man and they had just discovered that he knew a lot about the geography of Transoxiana. Jason was not the sort of person to undertake a venture without having first done considerable research into the project.

Jason explained, "Since the lockdown which came with the self-isolation imposed on the country to combat Covid, I've been able to work remotely from home like so many other people. I'll be able to continue my work when away, even as far as Kyrgyzstan, as I'll have a satellite link to my computer."

"Where will you be staying when in Kyrgyzstan?" asked Bill.

Becky had been waiting for this opportunity to tell her friends about her Kyrgyz penfriend.

"To help me study the language, I arranged to correspond with a penfriend in Kyrgyzstan who wanted to learn English. My penfriend in called Askari. Askari is a Baptist and she and her husband,

Temier, run a bookshop in a small town called Nann-Kol near Bishkek. Although not far from Bishkek, it's a fairly isolated community. Nann-Kol seems to be controlled by a fairly frightening character who styles himself, the Emir of Transoxiana, although he's nothing of the sort. When he's presiding at services in the Mosque, he's known as the Grand Mufti. Had he been a Shia Muslim, I think he'd have called himself the Grand Ayatollah. The way this Emir of Transoxiana teaches the Islamic faith is fairly extreme and the people of Nann-Kol seem to be in awe, if not actually afraid, of him. Askari and Temier sell Bibles translated into Kyrgyz in their bookshop and are really missionaries but don't describe themselves as such in view of the Islamic attitude towards proselytism. When I'm not working in Bishkek, Jason and I will stay with Askari and Temier. When in Bishkek, the Embassy will arrange my accommodation and they will help Jason in making arrangements to stay in a hotel. Fortunately, the cost of staying in a Kyrgyz hotel is very reasonable."

"Becky has studied Kyrgyz, but how will you cope with communication in this remote land with a strange language?" Bill asked Jason.

"Becky has taught me a bit of Russian and I hope to pick up Kyrgyz while I'm out there," said Jason. "As happened in Turkey under Ataturk, the Kyrgyz transliterated their written language from the very difficult Arabic script to Latin script. However, in the interest of extending Russian influence in the area, Stalin commanded the country to switch to Cyrillic script. This was a retrograde step as Cyrillic doesn't lend itself to Kyrgyz pronunciation as well as Latin script. It also adds to my difficulty in learning Russian. However, I understand that the Kyrgyz are still familiar with the Latin alphabet even if they can't remember the days before Stalin. A lot of them have computers with QWERTY keyboards. English is becoming an increasingly popular second language there as it is recognised as the lingua franca of the internet and they see a lot of American and British films. I think I'll get by in Kyrgyzstan."

Bill and Liz had a quick quiet word with each other and then Liz spoke out.

"You know how interested Bill and I are in hi-tech gadgets. Well, by coincidence, a couple of weeks ago, we discovered a device which you might find very useful in Kyrgyzstan. Let me go and fetch it. I only live a short distance away. I'll be back very soon."

Liz left the group and reappeared five minutes later with a small black box.

"This is a language translator," she said. "You load a memory stick programmed with two languages, say a sentence in one of those languages and after a few seconds, it speaks out a translation of what you've just said in the other language. It's not perfect but as far as we have been able to try it out, it works pretty well. It may take a little while to get used to a person's voice when it's being used. It will cope with languages like English, French, Spanish, German, yes, and it does Russian as well. Sadly, it doesn't do Kyrgyz. That's a development for the future. I'll load the box with English and Russian and we'll put it through its paces."

Liz inserted a pre-programmed memory stick and Jason, Bill and Liz said sentences in English, looking to Becky to see if the answering translations were accurate. Becky approved each time. She then said a few sentences in Russian and they found the machine responded with a reasonable English match. They then tried to catch out the machine, using some unusual English idioms and sayings. One of the sayings they tried was, "Out of Sight, Out of Mind." After a pause, the machine responded with just two Russian words. Becky fell about laughing. The other three looked puzzled.

"What did it say?"

Becky explained, "The two Russian words which came out were 'Blind Idiot'.

The others joined in Becky's mirth.

"What fantastic machine," exclaimed Jason. "It may still need some tweaking to become perfect but it could be a lifesaver to someone stranded in a country which speaks an unfamiliar language."

"Do take it with you to Kyrgyzstan," said Bill. "Although it can't manage Kyrgyz, it seems from what you say that a lot of people there speak Russian. It wasn't that expensive. We've both got good jobs and we're glad to be able to help out a friend embarking on what sounds like the adventure of a lifetime."

"I'm more than grateful to you both," said Jason, visibly touched by this generosity. "Having this device will go a long way in settling my anxiety about not being able to communicate with the Russian speakers in Kyrgyzstan. I'll make sure that I'm able to return it to you intact when I return."

Bill and Liz gestured to indicate that they didn't expect Jason to return it to them.

The foursome continued to chat for about another half-hour before Jason, Bill and Liz left to return to their homes.

So it was, a fortnight later, Becky and Jason set off on their journey to Bishkek in Kyrgyzstan. Bishkek, the capital of Kyrgyzstan, is a city with about one million inhabitants, that is just a little smaller than Birmingham. They had the various vaccinations recommended for travelling to that part of the world and boarded a flight from Birmingham International Airport. They had booked a flight with Lufthansa. As Becky was going on government business, her flight was paid for but Jason had to pay £330 for his ticket even though the Department of International Trade had indicated to Becky that she should find a companion to accompany her on this trip. They had to break their journey at Istanbul where they boarded an Emirates plane bound for Bishkek. They landed at Bishkek's Mana International Airport at about 9 o'clock in the evening. Jason and Becky were unable to fly direct to Bishkek from Britain as Kyrgyzstan has banned airline status. Kyrgyz safety standards fail to meet European safety requirements which means that no airline which is registered in Kyrgyzstan may operate services within Britain and the European Union.

They were met at the airport by an embassy official and driven in a very plush car to the British embassy. Accommodation had been reserved for Becky in the embassy. Jason was taxied in the embassy car to a hotel which the embassy had booked for him in Bishkek. The hotel was the Sara Boutique, a three-star hotel located not too far from the embassy. The Sara Boutique was a very pleasant hotel, offering all the usual facilities, air-conditioned en-suite rooms with flat screen television and wi-fi. Becky and Jason arranged to meet the following morning and use the two days allocated for Becky's acclimatisation to explore the city.

After both having spent a comfortable night in their separate locations, they met at the embassy as planned. They wandered along Chuy Prospekti, the main east-west street named after the River Chuy which flows by the city. Its former name, Lenin Avenue, harks back to the Soviet era. Becky had a map but the city was easy to navigate, its streets being laid out in a fairly rectangular grid. Although a mainly Muslim country, Russian influence is specially strong in Bishkek and Russian is the main language spoken in the city. Thus, one of the first sights they visited was the Russian Orthodox Cathedral of the Holy Resurrection. The main north-south street, Yusup Abdrakhmanov, was still commonly referred to by the name it had obviously been given in the Soviet era, Sovietskaya Street.

Sovietskaya Street appeared to be the best place to go shopping and the pair spent a lot of time wandering round the Dordoy Bazaar. The city was not short of inexpensive coffee shops and restaurants and just after midday they enjoyed a light meal of local fare. They decided that the city was a generally pleasant environment. Although there were a large number of Soviet era apartment blocks with fairly plain, utilitarian architecture, there were many other quite lovely buildings. Also, the streets were spaciously wide, characteristic of the way cities are designed in an environment where space is no object. They sauntered through the pleasant parks and well-manicured gardens, stopping to admire the many monuments although they didn't actually know what these monuments stood for or who were the personages represented by elegant statues. One of the statues in a park near the railway station commemorated Mikhail Frunze. Frunze was the former name of the city, dating back to a name imposed during the Soviet era. Mikhail Frunze was born in the city and was an important lieutenant of Lenin during the Russian Revolution of 1917. The city was renamed Bishkek when Kyrgyzstan became independent.

Besides the Russian Orthodox Cathedral, Jason and Becky were also able to admire the architecture of the Roman Catholic Cathedral and a number of impressive mosques. The main government building is called the White House. It was formerly the headquarters of the Kyrgyz Soviet Socialist communist party. This building can best be described as a huge, seven-storey marble block.

Jason and Becky browsed the State Historical Museum and the State Museum of Applied Arts. Becky translated for Jason the captions on the exhibits which were printed in both Kyrgyz and Russian. Ala-Too Square stands at a major road intersection and here, Jason and Becky viewed the changing of the guards ceremony by the Independence Monument.

After these couple of days sightseeing and acclimatisation, Becky had to start the work she had been sent to carry out so that over the next couple of weeks, Jason was left very much to his own devices while Becky visited various mining and industrial headquarters. These were both within Bishkek and in locations outside the city. Becky was conveyed to her meetings by an embassy car and was accompanied by a member of embassy staff to give her any help needed in translation where her Russian or Kyrgyz fell short in technicalities.

Jason spent his time well, making further sight-seeing excursions, carrying out language study and emailing Bill and Liz, his friends back in Britain, to keep them up to date with what was happening in Bishkek. He was able to let them know how useful the English/Russian translator that they had given him had been. Most days, he was also able to carry out his paid work from his hotel room without distraction, using his computer and satellite link. In the evenings, Jason and Becky were able to meet up for meals at various Bishkek restaurants.

At the end of a fortnight, Becky had done everything she could to pave the way for further trade negotiations to be carried out by more senior diplomats. She had built up a good contact list and accumulated details on commodities, costs and necessary transportation arrangements which would have to be made to facilitate the establishment of trade links.

Now was the time she could take the break which she had pre-arranged with her Kyrgyz penfriend, Askari and her husband, Temier, at the little town of Nann-Kol tucked away in the nearby mountains.

Chapter 4
Nann Kol

Having arranged the date that they would be coming to stay with her penfriend, Askari, Becky and Jason hired a taxi to Nann-Kol on the appointed day. Although only thirty kilometres from Bishkek, the journey took much longer than the couple had anticipated as the taxi wound its way around the narrow mountain tracks which they encountered soon after departing the outskirts of Bishkek. Ultimately, they arrived at their destination, paid off the taxi and turned to see a smiling Askari and Temier waiting to welcome them to their home.

Becky immediately recognised Askari from the photo she had received when they exchanged their pictures at an early stage in their correspondence. She was a plump, jolly looking woman dressed in traditional Kyrgyz costume, an ankle length white dress under an elaborately embroidered waist coat. Jason and Becky had noticed that many of the women they passed as they entered Nann-Kol were dressed this way. A significant number of them also wore the pointed hats which were part of the dress. Quite a few women could be seen wearing the hijab.

Temier was a good six inches taller than Askari and had the air of a very cheerful, easy-going sort of person. He stepped forward to help Becky lift her luggage into their small house and the pair showed Becky and Jason to their rooms on the first floor. These were sparsely furnished but looked to be very comfortable. Having deposited their bags and had a wash, Becky and Jason made their way downstairs where a meal had been prepared for them.

The first topic of conversation was their journey. They spoke mainly in Russian and by now, Jason could follow most of what was being said, Becky having to step in on occasions to help him when she realised he hadn't understood something. From time to time, they switched to English, Askari being anxious to practice her conversation skills in this language. On these occasions, it was Askari who had to translate on occasions for Temier's benefit, for although he had learned some English, he wasn't as proficient as Askari. Jason and Becky expressed surprise that their relatively short journey had taken so long. Askari held up her hands in exasperation.

"The roads in Kyrgyzstan leave a lot to be desired," she explained. "The roads near the borders are even worse in some ways. When they were built by the

Russians, no account was taken of national boundaries. I suppose they thought that one day, all these central Asian countries would become part of greater Russia. When you travel along these roads, your frequently find yourself crossing national borders with all the security formalities involved with that. The same applies to the railways. As a result, people tend to travel around on horseback rather than by train or car."

Becky and Jason had noticed large numbers of people riding horses as they approached Nann Kol.

"Equestrianism is very much part of Kyrgyz life," explained Askari, "and indeed, has been for centuries. That's specially the case in Nann Kol. It's easier to get around on horseback here than by car. We're a bit of an enclave, cut off from the rest of the country by the mountains around about and I sometimes think that the government has forgotten we're here."

The conversation then switched to their church.

"We're not doing badly for a church set in the middle of a predominantly Muslim society," said Temier. "We get at least twenty to our Sunday services but we're in touch with many more would be worshippers. We're winning converts but we have to be careful not to throw ourselves open to the charge that we're proselytising. Most of the people in the town are nominally Muslim and this is what they would state as their religion when filling in a form. The Mosques are fairly well attended. Some attend because there's not much else to do on a Friday but most of the worshippers are really devout. We're friends with a lot of Muslims and those we know who attend the Mosque are lovely people, leading exemplary lives."

Askari continued, "Being a fairly isolated town, there were very few cases of Covid in Nann-Kol during the pandemic. A few people had to ride over to Bishkek on business and vans came into the town to stack the supermarket shelves. No doubt, the infection came in through one of these sources but those infected were very good at self-isolating. No one was ill enough to require hospitalisation and everyone recovered. We Christians earned the approval of the rest of the community because we had the initiative to deliver food bags to every family who was self-isolating."

Temier returned to the religious situation, "The main problem we face with Islam comes not from the Muslim people but from the leader of their community, the self-styled Emir of Transoxiana. He's a frightening character, very fundamentalist in his outlook. He's served by a contingent of Islamic police. They're strict on dress code and woe betide a woman who is known to attend the Mosque if she's found not wearing her hijab. These police are for ever on the lookout for anyone consuming alcohol. They enforce strict segregation of the sexes in Mosques but there is nothing remarkable in this. It's the normal practice in Mosques the world over. The Emir's religious police come down very hard on any suspected of adultery. The gay lesbian community is an anathema to them and there aren't any openly gay individuals in Nann-Kol."

Jason asked, "Are there many prepared to serve in this religious police force?"

Temier shrugged his shoulders. "Recruiting new police doesn't seem to be necessary. Most of the existing religious police have been there ever since we moved to Nann Kol. However, a year or so back, the Emir's Islamic police were augmented by three men of Arab origin. It's strongly suspected that they were members of Isil and managed to flee Syria when Isil's last stronghold of Mosul fell. There's a Sharia court here in Nann-Kol which is regularly in session and a small prison where offenders against Sharia law are detained."

Askari added, "The Emir of Transoxiana wields considerable power through his religious police. The government doesn't seem to see the need to deploy regular civil police here because we're such a remote enclave. They know that this Islamic community is very law abiding and just leave it to the Emir and his religious police officers to maintain law and order."

Temier then explained the role of his shop in spreading Christianity in a way which wasn't seen as offensive to the Islamic community living in Nann Kol.

"Bibles are included among the books I sell at the shop and recently I've sold quite a number, even to those who attend the Mosque. The bookshop affords plenty of opportunities for witness without proselytising. I think the Muslims who've recently bought Bibles have been encouraged to do so by Kamalbek. He's a very articulate, well-educated Kyrgyz. He attended the Kyrgyz-Russian State University in Bishkek. Kamalbek came to Nann-Kol a year or so ago to help his father who was having difficulty in running his small holding as he advanced in age. Kamalbek is a Muslim and attends the Mosque but he's a liberal thinker and quite outspoken. He's brought a breath of fresh, outside air into Nann-Kol. He's very popular among the locals but doesn't get on so well with the Emir. I think this contributes to his popularity," said Temier with a smile.

The next few days were very exciting and interesting for Becky and Jason. They were introduced to a number of Askari and Temier's friends, both fellow church members and those from the wider community including Kamalbek. On Sundays, they attended services at Askari and Temier's Baptist church and really enjoyed the lively worship and friendly atmosphere created, even though they couldn't understand everything that was said. However, they felt themselves being made most welcome. At the mid-week prayer meeting, Becky and Jason were impressed by two of Askari and Temier's special friends, Nataldev and Felika Usenov. The language barrier didn't prevent Becky and Jason establishing instant rapport with the couple. Nataldev helped out at Temier's bookshop. He bore a strikingly similar appearance to Temier.

A couple of days later, Askari suggested that Becky and Jason should learn to ride horses, the main means of transport in that part of the country.

"When you return to Bishkek, you'll find the journey across country on horseback much quicker than the taxi ride you took to ger up here. When we go to Bishkek, we always go on horseback ourselves. We have an arrangement with a stable on the outskirts of the city by which we leave our horses to be looked after while we're in town and we collect them on our return journey. We can even leave the horses there for a few days. Not far from this stable, there's a trolley bus service which leaves for the middle of town every half-hour."

Becky and Jason were provided with a couple of lovely, docile horses and over the next few days, spent many happy hours learning to ride.

"This is fun," said Becky. "I'm going to take up riding when we return to the UK."

Chapter 5
The Emir of Transoxiana

The self-styled Emir of Transoxiana sat impatiently in the office adjoining the Nann Kol Mosque. He was a disagreeable looking man, his face bearing a permanent scowl. An unkempt straggly beard descended from his face in curly disorganised wisps of grey hair. He'd arranged by email to meet Kamalbek that afternoon. Email was the Emir's preferred form of communication. He wasn't a very sociable person and his ministry could hardly be described as pastoral. He didn't like to be kept waiting but he had no cause for complaint on that score on that day. The meeting was scheduled for three o'clock and it was now only ten minutes to three. At three o'clock precisely, one of the Mosque assistants knocked on the door and ushered in Kamalbek. The Emir gestured him to sit on the chair placed opposite his desk. Kamalbek looked defiantly at the Emir. One could immediately sense the antagonism.

"I gather that you've bought a Bible from the bookshop in town," accused the Emir.

"Yes, that's true but why should it be any concern of yours?"

The Emir bristled. "Of course it's a concern of mine. It's dangerous literature. It's the sort of book which can lead a Muslim astray!"

"In what way?"

"It contains teachings which are counter to the Islamic faith. It gives a false representation of Jesus. All you need to know of Jesus can be found in the Qur'an."

Kamalbek felt distinctly irritated by the Emir's assumption that he had the duty let alone the right to censor what people read and continued to defend his right to read the Bible.

"The Qur'an describes Jesus' virgin birth to his mother Mary and lists only six of his miracles. I rather think that Muhammad learnt about Jesus from a very inadequate source. How much better to go to a book written by first-hand witnesses who actually knew him as a person. I find the Bible accounts of the life of Jesus very plausible. Very little is found in the Qur'an of Jesus' moral teaching but as I read the Bible, I don't find any great disparity between his moral teaching and that of Muhammad."

"The Qur'an is not the invention of Muhammad," retorted the Emir in an exasperated tone. "It's entirely the word of Allah, revealed to Muhammad piecemeal by the angel, Gabriel, and Muhammad taught this revelation to his followers. It's a much more comprehensive revelation than anything received by Jesus. who lived eight hundred years before Muhammad. Thus, the teachings of Muhammad supersede those of Jesus. Jesus was only the penultimate prophet. Muhammad is Allah's ultimate prophet."

Kamalbek continued unabashed.

"Well, as I said, as I read the Bible, I was unaware of any of Muhammad's moral teaching which went beyond what Jesus had already proclaimed. There's a certain amount of teaching about ritual in the Qur'an, daily prayers, Ramadhan and the Hajj. Jesus doesn't major on ritual but tends to take the line that ritual is often no more than superficial. This difference shows up in the way that prayers are offered in the two faiths. When the faithful meet for prayer, they all bow in synchronism and listen to the prayer recited by the Mullah. I understand that at Christian services, there is provision for prayers to be led, both by the minister and ordinary members of the congregation. These prayers tend to be spontaneous and relate to current situations as well as including praise and confession"

"You're not aware of everything in the Qur'an. You need to hear more teaching from the Imams who have a detailed knowledge of the Qur'an to fully appreciate the teaching of Muhammad."

"Well, this is another problem I have with Islam," replied Kamalbek. "The Qur'an is not readily translated into other languages although I know that translations do exist but not in Kyrgyz. If it can only be read in Arabic, ordinary people are dependent on clerics to understand Islam."

"If you had any knowledge of Arabic and had attempted to read the Qur'an," countered the Emir, "you would realise what a special book this is and that it is not designed to be translated. That's why people, like myself, spend years in study to enable us to reveal Allah's word to people like yourself."

This answer didn't satisfy Kamalbek.

"Christian priests used to have this attitude about the Bible but in my European Studies course at university, I learnt about the European Reformation. During this period, the Bible was translated into the common tongues of people living in European countries and as a result, Christianity made great advances. They were able to ditch the false teaching they were receiving from their priests."

This line of reasoning seemed to attract the Emir's interest.

"What false teaching?" he challenged Kamalbek.

"Teaching about things like indulgences issued by the Pope," explained Kamalbek. "It was claimed that these indulgences would grant forgiveness of sins, not just those committed in the past but in the future. All this was bound up with false teaching about a place called purgatory which ordinary people were taught to dread and needed to buy indulgences to escape time there. Purgatory was a place invented by the corrupt church of its day to enable money to be raised through the sale of indulgences to good, well-meaning people who were taught that these were needed escape purgatory. The money was used to enrich the church. Some went on building projects but a lot of it found its way into clergy pockets."

"Well, doesn't this just make my point," responded the Emir, a rare smile crossing his face for the first time during this interview. "Christians are receiving false teaching from their priests!"

"Quite the contrary," answered Kamalbek. "Once Christians could read the Bible in their own language, they could discern that these doctrines had no place in what they regarded as God's word."

Kamalbek continued,

"By and large, Islamic clerics preach Qur'anic morality in a way which is quite acceptable but it's clear that what they teach is selective. They filter a lot of what is in the Qur'an. If the Qur'an could be read in the common tongue, ordinary Muslims who can't read Arabic, and that's most of us, would be able to learn so much more from the teaching of Muhammad."

"No, this wouldn't do!" exploded the Emir. "Only mullahs like myself who have spent years of study into the Qur'an are properly equipped and qualified to interpret its teaching to others."

"On the contrary," persisted Kamalbek. "I think that Islamic clerics hide a lot of Qur'anic teaching which many would find presented questionable morality. Unlike Christianity, Islam has spread through evangelism by the sword, in other words, if people who are conquered by Muslim armies don't become Muslims, they are slaughtered. Most of my fellow Muslims here in Nann Kol are appalled by the barbarity of the group which called itself Isil, slaughtering not only non-Muslims but those who didn't agree with their particular brand of Islam."

Kamalbek paused, waiting for a response from the Emir but it wasn't forthcoming so he continued.

"Surely, the Qur'an can't condone such behaviour, but it would seem that perhaps it does and Isil and other terrorist groups like Al Qaeda have been taught from the Qur'an, passages which justify killing and blowing up people, just because they're not Muslim, or who follow a different Islamic tradition. If some people can be persuaded that the evil they're being urged to do serves Allah, there's no limit to the amount of evil they will delight in carrying out."

The Emir picked up a Qur'an from his desk, thumbed through the pages, found the passage he wanted and then gave Kamalbek its translation.

"The Qur'an states

Qur'an 9:29 Fight those who believe not in Allah nor the Last Day, nor hold that forbidden which hath been forbidden by Allah and his messenger, and do not acknowledge he Religion of Truth, from among the People of the Book* until they pay the Jizyah with willing submission and feel themselves subdued.

*(*The 'People of the Book' in the Qur'an means 'People of the Bible' , i.e. Christians and Jews)*

So Kamalbek, beware becoming a Person of the Book!"

The Emir had unwittingly read a passage which supported Kamalbek's contention.

"Well, this is appalling," replied Kamalbek. "If my fellow Muslims knew that teaching from the Qur'an justified the appalling atrocities committed by groups like Isil and Al Qaeda, they would be most disturbed.

Another quite disgraceful thing which has happened not so long ago has been the murder by Islamic militants of journalists who worked for the French magazine, Charlie Hebdo, just because they took offence at a cartoon of Muhammad."

"Ridiculing Allah's prophet, Muhammad, is serious blasphemy and must not be tolerated," insisted the Emir. "Have you seen these cartoons?"

Kamalbek had to admit that he hadn't.

"Well" continued the Emir. "They're no Mickey Mouse cartoons. They're designed to be totally offensive in the way they ridicule Muhammad and by implication, the rest of Islam. Muslims believe that receiving Muhammad's support on the Day of Judgement is conditional on their defending him from abuse in their lifetime. Hence, the perpetuators of this form of blasphemy should have known that they were provoking a serious reaction from the faithful."

Kamalbek took a much more liberal view and replied, "Well, Muhammad's no longer around on earth to worry about a thing like a silly cartoon and neither should Allah be. Allah's a big God who's all powerful and who's been around for a long time. There are much bigger issues in the world for Allah to concern himself with. He doesn't need people, no, he doesn't want people to carry out evil acts which people suppose they are committing on his behalf. It would seem that for some Muslims, they are so lacking in both a sense of humour and of morality that they can't distinguish between a bit of harmless fun and brutal murder."

"Mocking the prophet isn't harmless fun. It's blasphemy!" exploded the Emir. "It has to be taken very seriously. As far as committing acts of evil, the Christians can be accused of doing much worse things than anything you find in Islam. Just look at the way they conducted the Crusades."

"There's no comparison. The Crusades were fought by Christians in the middle ages to protect the Holy Land from invading Islamic forces under war lords like Saladin."

The Emir changed the direction of the discussion.

"I gather the manager of the Nann Kol bookshop is called Temier Bivmok. When he sold you the Bible, did he attempt to convert you to Christianity?"

"No. He merely expressed to me the wonderful change that becoming a Christian had made to his own life."

The Emir mentally noted this. Kamalbek was unaware that this action of Temier's was sufficient by Shariah law to expose Temier to being charged with proselytization.

"I trust you're not considering becoming a Christian," continued the Emir. "You know the penalty for apostasy."

This time, Kamalbek bristled.

"How would you set about carrying out my execution? Getting some of these thugs you've recruited into your religious police to assassinate me? That would just create outrage among the Muslims here in Nann Kol and it would bring in the state police to deal with you in no uncertain terms.

This attitude is contrary to what is accepted as a basic human right. People should be completely free in their choice of belief. Religious leaders like yourself are free to persuade people to your way of thinking but not to force your beliefs with the threat of death! We're not living in the middle ages when only the clerics could read and write. We're living in a modern literate society where people are intelligent and discerning enough to decide for themselves what to believe. There is a saying which is common in many Mosques that 'Every Muslim should be a missionary.' Well, if it's OK for Muslims to be missionaries, why shouldn't Christians be missionaries too. Indeed many are but any who challenge Islam are persecuted."

The Emir didn't respond. He knew what Kamalbek had said was true. Kamalbek continued,

"Sadly, this is how Islam has survived in the way it has. Not only have people been threatened with death if they refuse to become Muslims, they know that technically, the penalty is death if they choose to leave the faith, although fortunately we don't have many examples of this in our modern day and age. No such sanctions exist in the way Christianity is practised today. Christians would be very sad if someone chose to leave their faith. They would try to win him or her back by persuasion but no violence would be offered. The person would still be an object of their love."

The Emir was lost for words. After a pause, he said,

"I think enough has been said today. I advise you to go away and think carefully about what I have said."

With that, he waved his hand as a sign he was dismissing Kamalbek from his presence. Kamalbek was tempted to suggest that the Emir should consider carefully things he had said but thought better of it and rose and left the Emir to himself.

Over the next few days, the Emir interviewed other members of the Mosque whom he had discovered had bought Bibles, some at Kamalbek's persuasion. In each case, he discovered that although Temier had in no wise tried to induce them to adopt the Christian faith, he had spoken enthusiastically of the wonderful change that becoming a Christian had made to his own life.

A day or so later, the Emir arranged to meet Ahmed al-Shayei, Kamal al Akaba and Qutaiba Attougui. These were the three Arabs who had arrived in Nann Kol a year or so earlier and had been immediately recruited into the Emir's religious police. The suspicions of the inhabitants of Nann Kol were well founded. These were indeed Isil fighters who had been able to escape from Mosul during the last days of Isil and made their way across central Asia to Kyrgyzstan. It wasn't clear at that point how they knew that they would be welcomed by the Emir who lived in Nann Kol.

The Emir explained to them the task which lay ahead.

"We have a serious case of proselytizing in Nann Kol. The perpetuator is Temier Bivmok who owns the town bookshop. He needs to be arrested and brought to trial when the Shariah court next sits. I need you to arrest him and take him to the prison by the Mosque. This primarily exists for religious offenders. I suggest that you wait near his house just before eight o'clock in the morning and arrest him as he sets off for his bookshop. There won't be a problem. Very few people will be out and about at that time."

The Emir then took out a detailed map of Nann Kol and showed his religious police the exact location of Temier's house.

<u>Chapter 6</u>
<u>The Shariah Court</u>

Temier set off for work as the sun was rising. It promised to be a fine day and Temier was looking forward to cataloguing the most recent assignment of books which had arrived at the shop. He was suddenly aware that he was surrounded by two men each side of him and one behind. The two each side of Temier grabbed his arms. Temier realised with horror that these were the recently recruited Arab members of the religious police. There were three of them and they were strong. It would be pointless to struggle to get free. Whatever was going on? Whatever had he done for this to happen?

"You're under arrest for proselytizing," barked one of the Arabs, speaking with a heavy accent.

"You can't arrest me," protested Temier. "I'm not a member of the Mosque. You have no jurisdiction over me."

Temier was ignored. He was taken to the prison by the Mosque and locked in a cell.

Temier was alarmed. He had heard of bad things which happen to those who offend Muslims with extremist views. What would happen to Askari? Will the members of my church be able to help me? Anxious thought started to endlessly circulate in Temier's head.

News soon reached Askari and as you might expect, she was most distressed. No, she was distraught. She sought comfort from Becky and Jason.

"As recently as 2014, a person was convicted in Morocco to thirty months in prison for proselytizing," she sobbed. "I know that that conviction was overturned by a Moroccan appeals court but who knows what sort of sentence this mad Emir will hand out. What he's doing is quite illegal by Kyrgyz law but the government doesn't seem to care what goes on in Nann Kol. There's no appeals court we can turn to."

A meeting was convened of the church elders. A deputation was sent to the Emir to protest but he refused to see them. Over the next few days, the situation began to clarify itself. Temier was accused of proselytizing and if found guilty, could face a lengthy prison sentence. What was the church to do?

Becky and Jason attended the meetings convened by the church elders and with the help of Becky acting as a translator, Jason gained a good understanding of what had happened. Each meeting of the elders was closed with a prayer session during which the members were urged to listen carefully to anything God might be saying about the situation. Jason felt inspired at one of these meetings. He needed to establish a few more facts.

It would appear that an hour was set aside each morning for the prisoners to meet with one friend. At these meetings, the prisoners and their visitors sat on opposite sides of a table in a fairly spacious room in the prison complex. The meetings were supervised by a small contingent of religious police, perhaps no more than two or three officers. The prisoners could be distinguished from their visitors because they were dressed in red prison jackets. Askari or a church member visited Temier during this meeting hour, every morning before the actual trial. A date had been set for the trial. Soon after his arrest, Temier had been joined in his cell be two Muslim friends who'd been arrested for consuming alcohol. They had a ready defence. They weren't drinking alcohol but only coke but the religious police who arrested them didn't seem to appreciate that coke was not alcoholic. To them, any drink imported from America was Satanic and therefore, bound to be alcoholic. However, Temier's friends would have to wait for the formal trial before this fact could be properly established and they could be released.

As Jason prayed, the facts that he had picked up during the meeting organised themselves in Jason's mind into a plan which just might work. As the time of intense prayer came to a close, Jason volunteered that he had received a plan which he believed would get Temier out of the prison. He warned Temier's friend, Nataldev, that his plan, if adopted, could put him at some risk and was dependent on the cooperation of Temier's cell mates.

The gathering then listened to Jason's plan. Becky, helped by Askari, translated as he spoke.

"Subject to Nataldev and Temier's cell mates agreeing, this is the plan which has come to me. Nataldev should be one of the next people to visit Temier. During the occasion that Nataldev visits Temier, provided they can exercise any choice where they sit, they should try to occupy a table as far away as possible from those occupied by Temier's cell mates and their visitors. At some point during the hour, Temier's cell mates would start an altercation between themselves which would issue in a scuffle. The guards would have to deal with this and during this diversion, Temier and Nataldev should change jackets and move to opposite sides of their table. Temier and Nataldev look sufficiently similar that the guards are unlikely to realise what's happened. Nataldev will return to Temier's prison cell at the end of the meeting. On returning home from prison, I suggest that Temier should remain in hiding until after we know the outcome of the trial. At the trial, it should be established that Nataldev is not Temier and there is no case to answer. The Emir will be left assuming his religious police have arrested the wrong man."

Those present murmured their approval and nodded their heads but it all depended on Nataldev. The company looked towards him to assess his reaction. It was very positive.

"What a brilliant idea," he enthusiastically responded. "I'd be glad to do anything to help my friend, Temier, and this will have the bonus of doing something which is really going to annoy the Emir. Yes, of course I'm game."

Needless to say, Temier's cell mates also enthusiastically endorsed the plan. They had no great love for the Emir and they greeted the plan in much the same way as Nataldev had done.

I don't need to describe the execution of the plan. It went exactly as Jason had suggested. They had an anxious moment as one of the guards looked closely at Nataldev as they returned to their cells but Nataldev defiantly returned the guard's stare. Nataldev looked sufficiently like Temier to deceive the guards. Nataldev returned to the cell with the two colleagues who had been arraigned on the charge of consuming alcohol to await the session of the Shariah court. This would be convened in a few days' time. Thus, Temier returned safely home where Askari had prepared a safe hiding place for him within the house in the unlikely event that the religious police might decide to search their home. However, there was no immediate danger of this happening.

Before the day of the trial, Askari received an email from Kamalbek, or rather, he forwarded an email from the Emir which had been sent to him to inform him that he was required to attend the Shariah court as a witness. Kamalbek stated above the message he was forwarding to Askari that he had no idea what he might have said about conversations he had had with Temier which might have thrown Temier open to the charge of proselytizing. However, at the trial, he would say nothing which might lead Temier to be convicted.

The day of the hearing arrived. Normally, the Emir would have been the presiding judge but as he was one of the litigants in this case, his deputy Mullah, Mustafa, was sitting as judge. Mustafa was a young Mullah and hadn't enjoyed working under the Emir but was in no wise intimidated by him. The first case to be heard was that of the couple who'd been arrested for drinking alcohol. This was quickly dismissed when the couple could produce the cans from which they'd been drinking. These had contained the non-alcoholic coke and the prosecution could produce no conclusive evidence that alcohol was being consumed.

The proselytizing case commenced with the required formalities. Mustafa checked that he had the documents giving the full names, occupations and places of residence of both the plaintiff and the defendant, the date the case had been submitted, and the court where the lawsuit had been filed. He reassured himself that he'd filed the subject of the case, together with the plaintiff's claim and the support for making this claim. He read these out but when Nataldev rose to protest, he was curtly told to sit down and allow the proceedings to take their course. Nataldev was no longer wearing the red prison jacket but the coat which Temier had been wearing when arrested.

Mustafa asked the Emir what evidence he proposed to present in pursuance of this case and was told that the witnesses would testify that Temier had sold them Bibles and tried to influence them to renounce Islam and become Christian by emphasising what a difference being a Christian had made to his life.

This seems flimsy but has been sufficient on other occasions to secure a conviction of proselytizing.

The first witness was called. In a Shariah court, all the questioning is carried out by the judge.

"Did you buy a Bible from the defendant?" asked Mustafa.

"No," replied the witness. "The defendant isn't Temier Bivmok, the name you read out in the formalities with which you opened this trial!"

There was a murmur round the court. Mustafa looked up. The Emir put on his glasses. He was short sighted but preferred not to use his glasses much. The Emir went crimson. Was this in anger or embarrassment? Indeed, the defendant wasn't Temier. His religious police had arrested the wrong man. Mustafa looked hard at the Emir. A silence descended on the court. The Emir started to shuffle the papers he had brought to court.

"Would you make a statement concerning the defendant," Mustafa challenged the Emir.

The Emir stood.

"This is not the intended defendant. Some dreadful mistake has been made. Dismiss the case."

This time, the murmur in the court was no longer a quiet humming and Mustafa had to demand silence. Mustafa glared at Nataldev.

"Why didn't you say you were not the intended defendant at the beginning of the case when I read out the defendant's name?" demanded Mustafa.

"I rose to do just that," replied Nataldev, "but I was told to sit down and wait my turn to speak."

Mustafa then declared, "Case dismissed. Release the defendant."

Nataldev strode defiantly from the court, trying to conceal a grin.

When they met in the official's room after the court had had been recessed, the Emir and Mustafa were both very angry but for very different reasons. Although junior to the Emir, Mustafa didn't mind speaking his mind to him as he vented his anger.

"What do you think you're doing?" he bellowed at the Emir. "You've made the Shariah court look ridiculous. You had no evidence to pursue the case against the couple accused of drinking alcohol and you had the wrong man arrested on the proselytizing charge. Didn't you think to check all this out before the court session? We've been able to run Nann Kol much as we liked without outside interference, but if this debacle gets back to the government, we'll have a contingent of civil police imposed on us and that will spell the end of any authority wielded by the religious police."

"It's just a matter of the religious police arresting the wrong men," the Emir meekly replied to his junior.

"Just a matter of wrongful arrest!" exploded Mustafa. "If the officers who carried out these arrests were those three Arabs you've recruited, get rid of them. The people don't like them. It's rumoured they are members of Isil who have escaped from Syria.

Well, we don't want that sort of person in Nann Kol!"

The Emir left the building fuming. Those Christians had tricked him. He'd get his revenge but how?

Chapter 7
Tashkent

Meanwhile, Becky and Jason received slightly disturbing news from back home. They had kept Bill and Liz updated by email with all that had been happening to them while in Transoxiana. Bill had asked them to forward the email from the Emir which had earlier been forwarded to Askari by her Muslim friend, Kamalbek. Why ever should Bill request this? Their answer came a few days later in an email from Bill. Bill had a good degree from Imperial College in Computer Science and was quite a wizard as far as computing was concerned. It was headed 'URGENT MESSAGE'.

'Hi Jason and Becky,

Thanks for keeping us up to date with all that's going on in Nann Kol. Congratulations on your plan to turn the tables on the Emir and avoid Temier having to face trial and probable imprisonment. Thanks too for forwarding Kamalbek's email to me. I had an idea about how I could use that email to discover things which might be important to keep you all safe. As the Emir's email address was on the email you forwarded to me, I was able to send the Emir an email which would have appeared to have come from the Arab news agency, Al Jazeera. It was an article about the political crisis in Somalia which I copied and added as an attachment. It's in English so he probably won't be able to read it and he won't have any idea why it was sent to him. However, I buried a bug in the attachment which became activated as he downloaded the attachment. I am now able to hack into the Emir's computer and I've had a look at his emails. I know this is illegal but I have no scruples about hacking the Emir's computer in light of the way he has treated your friend, Temier.

Well, it's just as well I have hacked into his computer. I browsed through his emails. He's sent most of these to his Arab contacts. I don't know if there's such a thing as a keyboard which will type Arabic but anyway, the Emir hasn't got one. What he's done is to write his messages in Arabic in long hand, scan the message and then attach it as a JPEG file to his email. I've copied most of his recent messages. Of course, I can't read them but Liz has a friend who's fluent in Arabic and she's got him to translate them for us.

The reason I headed the email, 'URGENT MESSAGE', is because the translations Liz has obtained of the Emir's messages indicate that he is absolutely furious about what went on in court and is planning some dire revenge although as yet, this is unspecified. I would therefore suggest that you and your friends get out of Nann Kol fairly soon. As the state police don't seem to be operating in Nann Kol and the religious police are under the control of the Emir, Temier doesn't stand much chance of being justly treated when the Emir puts into action whatever scheme he has in mind.

The Emir's email clearly indicated that he's in touch with an Isil group located in Uzbekistan and he has had correspondence with the former leader of Isil, Abu Bakr al-Baghadi. It's almost certain that the three Arabs in the Emir's religious police are Isil fugitives who knew that the Emir would offer them a safe refuge when they got away from Mosul when Isil in Syria was finally defeated.

I hope that this email is going to prove useful to you as you make your plans for the next stage of your time in Transoxiana. Keep in touch,

Bill

Jason shared this news with Temier and Askari. They decided to arrange a prayer meeting with other church members. That evening, they all met together and with the help of Becky and Askari, Jason was able to explain to them the content of Bill's email.

They prayed expectantly and at the end of the time in prayer, they shared what they had heard.

Becky explained that she would soon have to leave Nann Kol and move to Uzbekistan to continue with the work she had been sent to carry out in Transoxiana. She suggested that Askari and Temier should accompany them as they moved to Uzbekistan. Since the trial at the Shariah court, Temier had only left home in the company of several friends but this couldn't carry on indefinitely. At some stage the Emir would get him rearrested or worse. However, what would happen to Temier and Askari's house if they left Nann Kol.

Askari had the answer.

"I know that Nataldev and Felika are sharing a house with friends while their new house is still in the state of being build the other side of Nann Kol. They could come and live in our house while we're away and Nataldev could take over the running of the bookshop."

How very neat. Everyone approved of this idea. Nataldev and Felika were particularly enthusiastic. So plans were put into action to enable Temier and Askari to travel to Uzbekistan with Jason and Becky.

A number of formalities had to be sorted first. Temier and Askari needed passports with the necessary visas to travel between the central Asian republics. Accompanied by Jason and Becky, they rode into Bishkek. to obtain these. It took eight days for the necessary paperwork to be completed. They had to return to Bishkek to collect these documents but they now had all that was needed to set off. Becky had contacted the Embassy in Tashkent to make final arrangements for staying there while on her trade mission. As at Bishkek, arrangements had been made for Jason to stay in a hotel in Tashkent. This was the International Hotel, conveniently located near the Expo Centre and the International Business Centre and only twenty yards from the Bodamzor metro station which would facilitate travel round the city. Becky arranged for the Embassy to book an extra double room at this hotel. The responsibility for paying for this accommodation rested with Jason and Becky. Temier and Askari expressed misgivings about their ability to pay their share but Jason and Becky insisted that this was their treat. They said that this was small recompense for the wonderful hospitality they had enjoyed while staying in Nann Kol with Temier and Askari.

The day of departure arrived. Nataldev and Felika arrived to take over the house. Askari had arranged with a friend who had a van to drive them into Bishkek where they would take a bus to Tashkent. This journey was arduous. It took fourteen hours and, as was the case with so many central Asian roads built in the Soviet era with no thought for future international boundaries, it involved two border crossings, in and out of Kazakhstan. They had to vacate the bus at Zhibek-Zholu for the formality of visa and passport checks but they ultimately crossed into Uzbekistan and reached Tashkent an hour later.

The history of Uzbekistan is not dissimilar to that of Kyrgyzstan. It had been annexed to Russia in the time of the Czars and then, in 1920 it became a Soviet Socialist Republic. It became independent with Glasnost in 1990 but the transition was not without turmoil. Uzbekistan hosts a multi-ethnic society and inter-ethnic violence flared from time to time during the early days of independence. In these early days of independence, Uzbekistan's human rights record was very poor. It's not good today but the government is aware that this is a problem and hundreds of laws have been passed in the interest of improving human rights. Being multis-ethnic, several languages are spoken in Uzbekistan but by far the majority of the people speak Uzbek, a Turkic language, different from but similar to Kyrgyz. There is a significant Russian community in Uzbekistan and Russian is fairly widely spoken as an interethnic language. This gave Jason some confidence that he would be able to get by in Uzbekistan, even if Becky wasn't with him. He was already beginning to pick up a bit of spoken Russian and he had the language translator which Bill and Liz had given him which would hopefully be helpful where his own Russian was limited. Before 1920, the language had been written in a script known as Nasta'liq. As had been the case with Kyrgyz, the written language was recast to use a modified Latin alphabet but during the soviet era, Uzbeks had had to change to a Cyrillic script. Unlike the Kyrgyz, they had changed back to the Latin script after independence.

On arrival at the bus terminal in Tashkent, they were met by an Embassy official who dropped Becky off at the Embassy and then drove Jason, Temier and Askari to the International Hotel where their rooms had been booked. Becky arranged to meet them at the hotel the following morning and would use the couple of days she had been allocated for acclimatization for sight seeing with them. The hotel had all the facilities you would expect at a quality hotel, swimming pool, fitness centre, bar and free Wi-Fi. Temier and Askari were most impressed. They hadn't previously had the opportunity to enjoy such luxury.

The following day, Becky met them as planned. Jason and Becky had been impressed with Bishkek, but they found Tashkent to be an even more splendid city. Its early prosperity had arisen from the fact that it was an important stopping point on the silk route, the road used for trade between China and the Middle East. The roads were wide and spacious which was very much the result of Russian influence on city development. However, most of the drab apartment blocks and shops of the Soviet era had been replaced by buildings of more pleasing architectural style. There were lovely parks around the city centre and many beautiful mosques and Islamic shrines. Some of the most impressive buildings were madrassahs, that is, educational establishments where great emphasis was placed on Islamic learning and culture. One of the most lovely and impressive buildings visited by the foursome was the Amir Timur Museum. In England, Timur is usually referred to as Tamburlaine. He was a ruthless conqueror and during his life, built an empire which not only covered the huge central Asian region of Transoxiana but extended to Moscow in Russia,

Delhi in India, Damascus in Syria and into Egypt. Tamburlaine was about to invade China but his death set a limit to the eastern expansion of his empire. Although a conqueror in the Genghis Khan mould, slaughtering huge numbers in his genocidal rampage of conquest, Amir Timur is the Uzbek national hero. As in most cultures, successful war lords who bring their nations glory are held in great esteem, regardless of the suffering inflicted in their quest for the adulation which comes with great military victories.

There was a limit to how much sightseeing Becky could take in during the two days allowed for acclimatization but after Becky returned to her diplomatic duties, Jason, Temier and Askari continued to explore this fascinating city. One thing Jason enjoyed was being able to visit places of interest without having to compete with the tourist throng which crowd out so many places of interest in European cities. They found the State Museum of History as interesting as the Amur Timur Museum. The Kukeldash Madrassah and Dzuma Mosque were particularly impressive buildings of their type. They had a panoramic view of the city from the Tashkent TV Tower and took great pleasure in shopping at the Chorsu Bazaar. They enjoyed their midday meals at the Central Asian Plov Centre. In the evening, they met up with Becky for a stroll down the Broadway Boulevard to browse round the souvenir shops and be entertained by the street artists. They would stop for a snack at one or other of the many food outlets.

Becky had found her trade mission work more challenging than it had been in Kyrgyzstan. China rather than the West was seen as the nation's natural trading partner. Uzbekistan was rich in copper, gold and uranium as well as in oil and natural gas. These were all valuable export commodities. The country was more than self-sufficient in the generation of electricity. Becky had had some success in promoting Jaguar Land Rover products. They showed interest in the Range Rover vehicles and expressed particular interest in the all-electric car which was scheduled by Jaguar for production in the near future. While these would be out of the price range which ordinary people could afford, they were seen as prestige cars for senior government officials. Becky felt that agricultural equipment made by firms like Teagle and Farmster would find a market in Uzbekistan, particularly tractors, combine harvesters, balers, sprayers and dynamic finishing mowers. She would return to the UK, able to report some success in the mission to which she had been assigned.

Meanwhile, back in Kyrgyzstan, the Emir of Transoxiana was fuming and bent on vengeance for the humiliation he had experienced at the Shariah court. Where had Temier gone to ground? The news filtered through to him that Temier, his wife and two English friends were now in Tashkent. Jason had been readily noticed in Nann Kol as there were very few black people living in Kyrgyzstan. The Emir's three newly recruited Arab religious policemen could be assigned the task of wreaking the revenge the Emir desired. He explained to them what would be required but met with some resistance.

Ahmed al-Shayei was the first to object. "Where will we stay in Uzbekistan?"

The Emir was already prepared for this. "I'm in contact with a secret Isil cell in Uzbekistan. You can stay there. The address is very secret and must not be disclosed on any account!"

Kamal al Akaba raised another problem. "But how can we cross the border? We've no passports. In our journey from Syria to Kyrgyzstan to get here, we had to find ways through the porous borders of the countries we've travelled through and had to take immense risks."

The Emir was well aware that these documents would be needed but knew they couldn't be obtained through official channels for these Arabs. "I've got a contact in Bishkek who can provide you with forged passports and visas".

Qutaiba Attougui had another problem. "How are we going to locate the people you want us to? Tashkent is a big city. We've already made a mistake in our attempt to identify Temier when we arrested the wrong man"

The Emir realised that this was an obvious problem but again he had the answer. "Temier will be travelling with his wife and two English friends, a man and a woman. The Englishman is black. There aren't many black people in Tashkent. The woman works at the Embassy. Watch the Embassy. If you see four people coming out and one of them is black, those will be the people you're looking out for."

Ahmed al-Shayei asked,
"Which one will be Temier?"

The Emir held up his hands in exasperation at what he thought was a silly question. Was Ahmed just being silly or wilfully obstructive?

The Emir impatiently replied, "The one who isn't black!"

Qutaiba Attougui raised an important practical difficulty. "We're going to need money, a lot of money. Where'll we get that?"

This was something the Emir was prepared for. "No problem. I can let you have all the money you'll need."

Indeed, the Emir had access to considerable sums of money from the Mosque treasury. Because the Muslims at the Emir's Mosque didn't use normal banks, no proper auditing of Mosque accounts took place and the Emir dipped into the Mosque treasury whenever he needed funds. Unbeknown to his congregation, he had sent money to his Isil contact in Uzbekistan during the time that Isil was actively fighting in Syria.

It took only two days for the Emir's contact in Bishkek to forge passports for the three Arabs. He already had blanks from which Kyrgyz passports could be prepared. His services to produce these were often in demand. The three of them set off for Tashkent.

Towards the end of their stay in Tashkent, Becky was invited via the Embassy to attend a trade seminar with a friend. Thus it was arranged that Temier and Askari should have a day to themselves shopping and enjoying the short time remaining in this lovely Tashkent environment while Jason would accompany Becky to attend the seminar. Two Uzbek members of the Embassy staff would also attend the seminar to help Becky as translators,

It all happened so quickly. Jason, Becky and the two Embassy personnel were no more than twenty yards from the Embassy. Suddenly, they found themselves confronted by three sinister looking men of Arabic appearance. One of these, wielding a knife, stepped forward and lunged at the male member of the Embassy pair, striking him in the stomach. Jason immediately sprang into action. He struck the assailant on the jaw, sending him reeling. A second Arab approached, clearly intent on attacking Jason this time. He raised his knife, ready to bring it down on Jason. Jason was able to grab man's wrist with both his hands before the knife descended. Jason turned his back on the man, pulled the Arab's arm so that his shoulder was in the Arab's armpit and pulled the man's arm further down so that the man was thrown over Jason's shoulder, a throw known in wrestling circles as a flying mare. The man dropped his knife with a clatter as he fell winded in to the floor. Jason picked up the knife and looked towards the third man ready for action. This man was not prepared to risk attacking a knife-wielding Jason single handed. Jason could clearly handle himself well when confronted by an aggressor. The third Arab put his knife away, helped his associates to their feet and the three of them made their way through the crowd which had started to gather, drawn to the scene by the turmoil being created. No one dared make any attempt to apprehend these knife wielding attackers and they quickly disappeared from view.

The man from the Embassy was lying on the floor, bleeding quite profusely from the wound he had received. Jason was bleeding slightly too from a superficial wound he had received on his neck during the scuffle. An ambulance was called. The four of them found themselves in the hospital, the two men having their wounds dressed. The man from the Embassy's wound was not considered to be life threatening but it was arranged that he should stay overnight in the hospital for observation. Jason's wound was properly dressed and not deemed serious enough to require him to remain in hospital. The police arrived to take statements. Becky described in detail what had happened. She stated that she recognised the assailants as members of the religious police in Kyrgyzstan who had tried to arrest a friend of theirs there a few weeks earlier.

The next day it was headline news in the Uzbek newspapers.

'Terrorist attack in broad daylight in Tashkent.

The assailants are believed to be religious extremists from neighbouring Kyrgyzstan.
It is not believed to have been racially motivated or an attack aimed at British personnel.
It is thought that the assailants misidentified their subject.
Heroic action by a young Englishman saved the life of the supposed targeted victim.'

The following day, the incident received coverage in the world press.

That evening, Temier and Askari were told about the incident and were most concerned. Jason and Becky laughed it off as all in a day's work, a characteristic piece of understatement. Two days later found them on the high-speed train from Tashkent to Samarkand on the next stage of the vacation which Becky had worked into her mission to Transoxiana. Jason and Becky had discovered that Bill and Liz had holiday due and so they invited them to join them in Samarkand.

Chapter 8
Samarkand

It was while still in Tashkent, that Becky and Jason decided that it would be a lovely idea if Bill and Liz could join them for the last part of this trip to central Asia. Having completed her trade mission work, Becky could now enjoy this as a holiday. Their suggestion was enthusiastically accepted by Bill and Liz as Covid restrictions of the previous year had prevented their having a proper holiday. So it was, Becky and Jason booked three double rooms at the Hotel Suzani in Mir Said Baraka Street, one room for Jason and Bill, another for Becky and Liz and the third for Temier and Askari. The hotel wasn't too far from the city centre and boasted of being multilingual which was considered to be a fairly important feature as only Becky knew enough Uzbek to get by in that language. However, as with most of Uzbekistan, Russian was a Lingua Franca used to enable interethnic communication. Jason was beginning to become proficient in Russian and he had the fallback of his computerised translator. While not as luxurious as the International Hotel in Tashkent, the Hotel Suzani wasn't expensive and more than adequate as a headquarters for a sightseeing holiday. Due to the uncertainty about the times of travel connections on Bill and Liz's journey and the time they would actually arrive in Samarkand, they arranged to meet at the hotel. Bill and Liz accessed the hotel by taxi from Samarkand International Airport. They had broken their journey at Istanbul, flying the final leg with Turkish Airlines.

On their arrival, they rendezvoused at the hotel as planned and Becky and Jason took great pleasure in introducing their friends to Temier and Askari. After allowing time for Bill and Liz to unpack, they set off for the nearby Restaurant Platon. Over their meal, Jason and Becky were able to fill them in on all the details of their exciting trip which they hadn't already shared in their email correspondence. Particular concern was expressed about the attack in Tashkent but Jason glowed in the praise poured on him for being such a hero on that occasion.

The next few days were spent exploring Samarkand, Tamburlaine's (Timur's) capital, from which he conquered large swathes of central Asia. Like Tashkent, Samarkand had been a very important stopping point on the Silk Route. Becky and Jason had been impressed with Bishkek, even more with Tashkent but Samarkand was really something else. It was absolutely magnificent with its impressive mosques, madrasahs and mausoleums. Russians had been involved in the development of Samarkand during the time of the Czars and Christian places of worship were also in evidence. They visited St. John the Baptist's catholic church and the Armenian Church. They were particularly impressed by the St. Alexy Moscowsky Orthodox Cathedral. In the absence of a Baptist church, they decided that they would attend this cathedral for their Sunday worship. The service was quite different from anything they'd experienced in churches before. It appeared that there weren't set service times but the service continued through the day with officiants changing and worshippers coming and going at different times throughout the service. The service was largely conducted in Russian but Jason and Becky were only able to pick up parts of this. However, the atmosphere of worship was profound. All of them considered that they'd never heard better choral music.

As they explored the city, the Registan Ensemble which consisted of three huge madrasahs arranged around three sides of a square, was a particularly impressive sight. They discovered that these were the Ulugbek Madrasah, the Tilya Kon Madrasah and the Sher Der Madrasah. Nearby was the Ulugbek Observatory. They visited the Guy Emir Mausoleum were members of Tamburlaine's dynasty are buried and also the shrine of Timur and Timurida. They decided that the most impressive mosque was the Bibi Khanum Mosque, named after Tamburlaine's (Timur's) wife. They had noticed that blue and gold were the predominant colours in which these great buildings had been decorated. It would appear that these were colours of significance in Samarkand. They learned a lot about Uzbekistan as they painfully deciphered the captions on the exhibits in the Regional Studies Museum and the State Museum of the Culture History of Uzbekistan. They punctuated their sightseeing forays with frequent visits to the Blues Café, located quite near their hotel and spent time relaxing in the city parks. It was an idyllic existence.

Meanwhile, in Nann Kol, the Emir had read the news of the abortive attack which his three Arab fugitives had carried out in Tashkent and realised that the finger would soon be pointing at him as the one responsible for initiating this. State police would descend on Nann Kol and he would have difficulty in convincing them that he hadn't orchestrated this attack. He needed to get out of Nann Kol and join the three Arabs at their Isil safe house in Uzbekistan. Three days later, he left Nann Kol and arranged for his deputy, Mustafa, to take over the Mosque while he was away.

A fortnight into their stay in Samarkand, the three ladies had gone out on a shopping excursion leaving the men relaxing in the hotel. They returned in a state of high anxiety. They reported to the men that they had seen the Emir and his three Arab associates walking in the Central Park, stopping every now and then apparently to make enquiries of people they met walking through the park. Fortunately, they themselves had not been spotted and they had returned immediately to the hotel. What action should they take?

No one had a ready answer and they decided that they would first pray and then go and think about what to do. They still had ten days left of the stay they had planned in Samarkand. They went away to separately think about what would be the most judicious course of action before returning to pool their thoughts.

They met to confer together an hour later.
"Cut short our holiday immediately," was one suggestion.
"Move to a hotel on the outskirts of the city," was another.
"Just carry on as if they weren't there," was also suggested.

Bill came up with the most constructive suggestion. He had spent the hour surfing his computer and could describe in some detail the plan he'd come up with from the information he'd gleaned.

"Why should we let these criminals ruin our holiday. I think we've seen most things of beauty and interest in Samarkand so let's leave this city for a few days to have an alternative holiday experience. I've discovered something very different we can do which could be very exciting. From Samarkand, we can reach Nukus, a city in the north of Uzbekistan, by rail. I don't think that Nukus itself is of great interest but from Nukus, camel treks are arranged, travelling by what's left of the River Oxus to the Aral Sea and beyond into Kazakhstan. A trek lasts about a week. We can return to Samarkand for a couple of days and then start our journey home and I suggest we travel to Istanbul via Diyarbakir in eastern Turkey."

None of them had heard of Diyarbakir but Bill seemed to have researched this well and his was the only plan for which all of them had shown enthusiasm. This seemed really exciting. So it was, they arranged with the hotel to leave the following day to travel north to go camel trekking but would return in a week for a couple of days before travelling on to Diyarbakir on their journey home. They asked if they could leave any possessions they wouldn't need on a camel trek in a safe place in the hotel. The hotel was more than accommodating. It wasn't busy and had few bookings for the next few days. Provided they left their rooms tidy, they could leave any possessions they didn't want to take camel trekking in their rooms and collect them when they returned for their final two days in Samarkand.

Bill arranged with reception to enter into their register that on leaving Samarkand, they would be staying in Diyarbakir specifying a false date. Why had he done this? Bill was very canny and he had this information entered into the hotel register on the basis of a strong premonition he had about the way things might turn out. Bill made arrangements for the party to join the camel trek on his computer and the following day, they set off for Nukus.

While they were away, an unsavoury incident occurred at Hotel Suzani. Two days later at 3:00 a.m., four men entered the hotel and demanded the hotel night shift receptionist who'd been drowsing at the reception desk, to tell them which room was occupied by Temier Bivmok. Of course, the receptionist refused. The four men came round the desk, one of them held a knife at the receptionist's throat while the older one of the quartet found the hotel register and thumbed through it until he found what he wanted. He took the key to the room he had identified as that occupied by Temier and three of them went off to the lift, leaving one of their number threatening the receptionist with a knife. In ten minutes, they were back demanding to know why Temier's room was unoccupied. The receptionist said quite truthfully that he'd absolutely no idea. The older man looked through the register again and the three of them then left as suddenly as they'd arrived. The receptionist immediately phoned the police who responded about a quarter of an hour later but the four men were nowhere to be found. There seemed to be little doubt that these were the people who had been involved in the assault at Tashkent.

Chapter 9
Nukus

The population of Nukus is around three hundred thousand which makes it comparable to Coventry. The group were not initially impressed with Nukus. As the train entered the city, they found the view from the train window to be very drab. Indeed, in the Soviet era, the city could indeed have been described as a remote, sad and sombre metropolis. However, since Uzbekistan had become independent of the Soviet Union, a considerable amount of work has been undertaken to improve the ambience of the city. The broad streets which are a positive legacy from Russian urban planning were still in place and the large Soviet style city buildings had largely been replaced by brighter, more attractive edifices. The group revised their initial impressions as they walked into the city centre from the railway station and were able to appreciate the more recently erected buildings which were really quite pleasing to the eye. There wasn't much to do in Nukus. Not that this mattered as they weren't planning to stay in the town. However, they did have time to visit the Museum of Art which was really quite special and might be described as the jewel in the city's tarnished crown. They had a quick look in the city's bazaar and enjoyed a drink at the Cinnamon Café before it was time to take a taxi to the site from which the camel caravans would set off.

This brief acquaintance with the city centre and the people they met shopping and drinking in the café left them feeling that really, the city was a friendly place with some very cheerful and pleasant inhabitants. From the research he had done in planning this trip, Bill told them that sadly, the people still lived under the cloud of the unfortunate legacy of the Soviet era. Because of its remoteness, the Red Army had identified this as the place where they would set up their research unit for developing chemical weapons, that most dreadful type of warfare. It was in this unit that the terrible nerve agent, novichok, was tested. This became notorious in the United Kingdom as the poison used by the Russians in the attempted murder of the double agent, Sergei Skipol and his daughter, Yulia. The agents who carried out this attack carelessly discarded the bottle containing this toxin so that it caused Dawn Sturgess and Charley Rowley who picked up this bottle, to fall ill and Dawn subsequently died. A police officer, Detective Sergeant Nick Bailey, who was involved in helping Sergei Skipol and his daughter, became seriously ill and still didn't feel fully recovered for many months after being infected. Salisbury was subjected to a year long clean up in order to become properly decontaminated.

Toxic waste from the Nukus research unit, including anthrax, had been deposited on an island in the Aral Sea. As the Sea dried as a result of ill-conceived irrigation schemes which diverted its feed from the River Oxus (Amu Darya), this contaminated island became part of the mainland. This created the potential for the toxins to spread beyond the confines of what had been an island in the Aral Sea. The inhabitants of Nukus are now subject to wind borne salt and pesticides, blowing into the city from the dry bed of the former Aral Sea, causing respiratory disorders, cancers and birth defects. A further unfortunate outcome of interference with the flow of the Oxus, is that fishing was no longer available to contribute to the economy of Nukus.

After an all too brief look round the town, the group took a taxi to the site on the edge of the city where the camel caravans were organised. They weren't the only tourists embarking on this adventure. A group of about twenty Americans were already there, getting settled into the tented accommodation which had been provided. The tents would travel with them and provide shelter during their overnight stops. They were met by the cheerful, friendly leader of the camel drivers. He showed them the tents which had been allocated to them. They were rather more complex than the ridge or bell tents with which we're normally familiar. He could speak some English and assured them that his team would be responsible for dismantling, packing and erecting the tents as they left or reached their overnight stopping points. He then took them to introduce them to the camels. Each of them had been assigned their own camel. These were not Arabian camels, often referred to as dromedaries, but Bactrian camels from the Gobi Desert of Mongolia. Unlike their Arabian counterpart, they had two humps. The ladies in the group immediately fell in love with these huge beasts. They nonchalantly chewed as they surveyed the humans whom they would be carrying on this journey, with what appeared to be a supercilious air. They looked really good natured and appeared to be conveying the thought,

"If you treat me with respect, I'll do most things for you within reason but I don't do anything in a hurry. If you try to force me into doing something I don't want to, I won't!"

Liz really found these animals to be quite amusing creatures.

"Did you know," she said to Becky, "that a camel has been described as a horse designed by a committee?

Becky continued to survey her camel with admiration.

"Well," she replied, "I rather think that committee did a very good job1"

It was now getting late and the evening was drawing in. The camel drivers had prepared a meal for them and they took the opportunity of getting to know their American fellow travellers as they sat round a huge bonfire and shared this meal.

They awoke with the sunrise after a good night's sleep, washed with the basins of water the camel drivers brought round to them. They then gathered in a big circle to eat the breakfast served up by the camel drivers. They carried on chatting to their new American friends while the camel drivers loaded the pack camels with all that would be needed for the trip. The leader of the team took them aside to give instructions on how to mount and dismount a camel, and how to control the beast when in motion. He warned them that at the end of the first day, they would probably feel saddle sore but they had arranged for fairly soft cushioning to be placed between the camels humps to make their seating as comfortable as possible.

It was now time to mount their camels which they achieved without too much difficulty and then they set off. The caravan consisted of about fifty camels plodding along in an orderly file. Some of the camels were being ridden by the tourists whilst others carried baggage. The first part of the trek followed the River Oxus (Amu Darya) whose course was to the west side of Nukus. It was sad to see the water in the river being depleted as it was syphoned off at various points along its length to feed the irrigation schemes needed for the cotton fields. Liz was specially disappointed when they reached what was left of the Aral Sea and the Oxus was no more than a trickle. She still entertained romantic notions about this part of the world where ancient Greeks and Persians, Mongols and Tartars, under the charismatic leadership of figures like Alexander the Great, Genghis Khan and Tamburlaine (Timur) fought for supremacy. Another river, the Syr Darya flowed into the north end of the Aral Sea but didn't carry sufficient water to keep the Sea replenished. An attempt had been made to replenish the sea by building a dam, but this had failed when the dam collapsed. Parts of the Aral Sea were now a ships' graveyard where boats had been left stranded by the receding waters of the Aral Sea.

The land between Nukus and the Aral Sea is known as the Desert of Karakalpakstan. The word desert usually conjures up images of an endless stretch of sand as far as the eye can see, punctuated by barren rocks where the sand hasn't been blown into steep dunes. The Karakalpakstan Desert is in no way as bleak as this. Well separated tufts of spiky plants are found which seem to have sprung from the grey earth. Large swathes of green grass are frequently encountered where sheep and goats graze. Occasionally, a glimpse is caught of a lizard or marmot scurrying by. Sometimes, a coiled snake can be seen, basking on a rock. Eagles soar overhead.

The caravan crossed into Kazakhstan and continued northward from the Aral Sea. The land became increasingly green as they entered the Steppes. This huge expanse of grassland, stretching to the horizon where distant hills could be perceived in some directions, corresponded closely with Liz's romantic view of a land where ancient armies of equestrian horsemen roamed. Bill mused on a different army, that of Hitler's troops carrying out Operation Barbarossa. He was well read and had a fairly good knowledge of the Second World War. He knew how dispirited the Nazi troops had become, travelling day after day across the Steppes into Russia, initially meeting very little resistance, destroying villages along the way and massacring their inhabitants lest they should interfere with the army's lines of communication, but seeing no sign of the objectives they were trying to reach. When an objective like Stalingrad was ultimately reached, the lines of communication were so extended that the army couldn't be reliably supplied and had to surrender.

After the time they had recently spent intensely sightseeing in Tashkent and Samarkand, this trip provided the extended time of relaxation they needed, daydreaming as their mounts gently and silently plodded on their way. Being desert animals, they seemed to know where the next watering place was located and were able to direct themselves there without needing to be guided by the experienced camel drivers. At these watering points, the travellers would leave their mounts to drink and the silence would be broken as the travellers enjoyed each other's company, relating stories and sharing experiences as they partook of their own refreshment. Each evening, the camel drivers would serve them with a light meal round a campfire while the tents were erected. As the night finally drew in and the stars came out in a cloudless sky, they would find their tents and sink soundly into deep sleep as the crickets created a gentle background sound.

After three days, they set off on the return journey by a slightly different route which took them past the ancient tombs of the Nizdakhan Necropolis, finally returning to Nukus. They warmly thanked those who had conducted the caravan and had given them a very different and enjoyable holiday experience. They then caught the train back to Samarkand. They were disturbed on reaching Hotel Suzani to hear of the night intrusion by a group whom they realised were the Emir and his three Arab associates. They were told that extra night watch staff were now on duty in view of this incident. They realised that Temier was the intended victim. These staff would be stood down when they left Samarkand.

Two days later found them on the next stage of their trip home. They boarded a train at Samarkand which travelled along the Trans Caspian railway to its terminus at Turkmenbashi on the Eastern coast of the Caspian Sea. As they made the connection to the ferry which would take them across to Baku, the capital of Azerbaijan, on the western coast of the Caspian Sea, they were impressed to see what a busy seaport Turkmenbashi was. Although, on a large scale map, the Caspian Sea may not look that big, it's the world's largest inland sea with no connection to an ocean. For most of the voyage across the sea, the party was completely out of sight of land. Baku was not on their itinerary for sightseeing but they couldn't avoid catching sight of the three spectacular towers in the city, the Flame Tower, the Socar Tower and the Sofaz Tower, as they took a taxi to the airport. Here, they caught the Turkish Airlines plane to Diyarbakir for which Bill had made bookings.

Chapter 10
Diyarbakir

While it may have been cheaper to travel to Diyarbakir overland, Bill had advised the group to fly there from Baku in view of problems which might have arisen in crossing borders The route would have taken them into Armenia and the relationship between Azerbaijan and Armenia was very tense.

Diyarbakir, a city of about one and a half million inhabitants and located on the River Tigris, is the de facto capital of Kurdistan. However, unlike the other 'stans' the group had recently visited, Kurdistan is not an independent country. Like Lapland which covers a large area across northern Scandinavia, the Balkans in the Eastern Mediterranean and indeed, Transoxiana, Kurdistan is a geographical area which embraces more than one country. It includes parts of eastern Turkey, northern Syria, northern Iraq and north-western Iran but is not itself a sovereign country. It was on the verge of becoming an independent state by the Treaty of Sevres in 1920 but the nation states who were reluctant to lose what they regarded as their sovereign territory failed to ratify this treaty and it remains a semi-autonomous region within the territories of the surrounding nations. A hostile relationship exists between the Kurds and the Turkish government. The majority of the inhabitants of Diyarbakir are Kurds but there are sizeable Armenian and Assyrian Christian communities.

Our six friends took the three and a half mile taxi ride from the airport to the Miroglu Hotel in the city centre where three rooms had been pre-booked. It was only a moderately comfortable establishment but adequate for the short stay our friends had booked. It had a three-star rating and the usual facilities including free Wi-Fi and a spa centre. Although it claimed to have air conditioning, this was turned off at night which left the rooms a little too warm for comfort. The feature which attracted Bill, who made the booking to this particular hotel, was its claim to be multi-lingual.

Bill and Liz had not done as much sight-seeing as the other four on this holiday and their time in Samarkand had been cut short. However, they were able to make up for this over the next couple of days. The city was surrounded by city walls which incorporated eighty-two watch towers. Access to and from the city centre was afforded by four wide gates. Further protection for the city, needed in mediaeval times, was provided by an impressive fortress.

The city was a bit of an anti-climax after the splendours of Samarkand but there were nonetheless some quite impressive churches and mosques. The most impressive mosque was the Sheikh Matar Mosque with a four-tiered minaret. The most significant church was the Syriac Orthodox Cathedral dedicated to the Virgin Mary.

A very important feature of Diyarbakir is found in the Hevsel Gardens, located between the Diyarbakir Fortress and the River Tigris. These are not ornamental gardens but a horticultural area used by the citizens of Diyarbakir to cultivate vegetables including cabbage, spinach, lettuce and onions, and fruit like grapes, melons and apricots. Numerous poplar trees grow in the gardens and some of the fruit is cultivated in orchards. Located near the gardens is the Dide Bridge which crosses the River Tigris. This was built in the eleventh century and encompasses no fewer than ten arches.

The only museum in the city which the friends found to be of interest was the Archaeological Museum.

Three days later, the friends caught a flight to Istanbul on the first leg of their journey back to the United Kingdom. At Istanbul, they had just enough time to look at the exteriors of the Topkapi Palace, the Hagia Sophia and the Blue Mosque. The Hagia Sophia is now again a mosque but was formerly the largest cathedral in the world and for a while, became a museum. The Blue Mosque is so named because of the predominance of blue Iznic tiles which decorate its interior.

Chapter 11
Back in England

Not knowing the actual date they would travel back to the United Kingdom, return flights had not been reserved but they had no problem booking a flight back to Birmingham International Airport with Lufthansa, the airline with which they had made their outward journey. On landing, they passed through the usual arrival procedures without delay and collected their cars from the long stay car park. Costs of airport parking are scandalously high but that's part of the modern world in which we live. Jason and Becky had travelled together to the airport as had Bill and Liz so there were only two cars to be located. They then set off for their homes in Easingdale. Temier and Askari travelled in Jason's car. He dropped Becky and their friends at Becky's parents' spacious home where she had arranged for them to stay during their time in England. After all the travelling they had done in recent days, all six of them felt fairly exhausted and the next couple of days were spent resting up. Even though it had been possible for all of four of the English young people to do a certain amount of their paid work by computer link, even while away in central Asia, they knew that they had quite a bit of catching up to do. However, they still had unused leave to take and this could be well used in showing Temier and Askari around England.

To make best use of their remaining leave, it was decided that on weekdays, they could take it in turn to show Temier and Askari round different parts of England which were well worth seeing. They would all make excursions together during the weekends. On the first day of sightseeing, Becky took them for a drive round the nearby Cotswolds This included a cream tea at Bourton-on-the-Water. A few days later, Liz took them to visit Kenilworth with its ruined but impressive castle in the morning, and in the afternoon, they moved on to explore Warwick and its intact riverside castle. The following week, Bill took them to Stratford-upon-Avon where they enjoyed looking round the souvenir shops and visiting Shakespeare's birthplace. Shakespeare was not an unknown person to the inhabitants of Kyrgyzstan. They loved the Tudor style buildings. Their visit included a river trip along the Avon. A week later, Jason took them to visit the lovely Jacobean mansion at Charlecote where they wandered along the river and took delight in watching the herd of wild deer grazing by the river. Weekday excursions included a trip to the Peak District, the Black Country Museum and Coventry

Cathedral. In Coventry, they were fascinated by the statue and story of lady Godiva.

By now, Temier and Askari were becoming quite proficient in spoken English and felt confident enough to make their own way around unaccompanied, revisiting parts of the Cotswolds and the Peak District. They made an independent visit to Leicester where they not only enjoyed the shopping experience but followed the suggestion that they should visit Leicester Cathedral. An adaptation of Shakespeare's play, Richard III, was known to them in Kyrgyzstan and they found the story of the discovery of the King's remains in a car park, the Richard III Museum and the associated shrine in the cathedral absolutely fascinating. What surprised them most was the way Richard III was portrayed in the museum as a good King. That evening, an interesting discussion was held with their hosts about the true nature of Richard III. Was he really the archvillain portrayed by Shakespeare or did he have redeeming features? Becky had to admit that the jury was out on whether Richard was really a good or a bad king. However, she explained that being a playwright, working during a period when there was controversy about whether or not the Tudor dynasty had a right to the throne, Shakespeare's play was a welcome piece of propaganda, blackening the image of the House of York and any in that family who may still have had pretentions to the crown. It would also have enhanced the regard with which Elizabeth I, the queen during the time of Shakespeare, would have held the playwright.

During the weekends, Jason, Becky, Bill and Liz were all free to accompany Temier and Askari on more distant excursions. They spent a long weekend in London, staying at a cheap hotel in Hampstead and travelling into the city centre by the London Underground. I can hardly list the multitude of historic sights, churches and museums they visited. The Houses of Parliament, Buckingham Palace and the Tower of London were all places with which Temier and Askari were familiar from pictures they had seen in travel books. At the end of this weekend, Temier and Askari had what might be called sightseeing indigestion and just wanted to spend the next few days, quietly visiting parts of the countryside they were coming to love.

A fortnight later, they all went on another major sightseeing excursion to York, that most historic of English cities. This time, they found an affordable hotel near the city centre. Unlike London, York was a city about which Temier and Askari knew absolutely nothing. They walked round the city walls, visited the Minster, browsed the Castle Museum, climbed up to the Clifford Tower and looked round the Railway Museum. York was a city they fell in love with at first sight.

Temier and Askari had kept in touch with Nataldev and Felika who were occupying their house while they were away. The news that came back was generally good. Both the bookshop and the church were doing well. After the news of the attack at Tashkent, which was obviously carried out by the Emir's religious police, was received in Nann Kol, a number of former Muslims including Kamalbek had abandoned the Islamic faith and joined the church. Nataldev and Felika let them know that their new house was now almost completely built.

The time was rapidly approaching when Temier and Askari knew they would have to return home and their anxiety levels started to rise. What might the Emir and his religious police have in store for them?

<u>**Chapter 12**</u>
<u>**The Interrogation**</u>

The Emir and his three Arab religious police arrived at Diyarbakir on 14th September, two days after our friends had departed on their homeward journey. Bill had shrewdly reckoned that the Emir would be spurred on by his recent failures to exact his revenge and would follow them to Diyarbakir. Expecting that the Emir would try to track them down, Bill had left the wrong date in the Samarkand hotel register. Although the Emir had not been able to find Temier when he raided the hotel, he had noted the information in the register and set off on this false trail as a result of that misinformation. They didn't follow the same route to Diyarbakir as our friends who had gone via the trans Caspian railway but flew direct from Samarkand. The Emir had left it to the last minute to travel to Diyarbakir as he had decided it was wise to stay in his Isil safehouse for as long as possible. In the event, Bill need not have worried about the group being traced in Diyarbakir as the Emir received a different reception at the airport from the one he had expected.

Whereas the fairly lax security on the Kyrgyzstan-Uzbekistan border, which large numbers of casual travellers were traversing daily, had enabled them to easily slip through with forged passports, things were very much tighter at the border check in Diyarbakir Airport. It wasn't so much that they were entering Turkey but they were arriving at the part of Turkey controlled by the Kurds. In view of the recent conflict which Isil had waged against the Kurds, the Kurds were still on high alert.

The Emir, travelling under his actual name, Natalya Almazbekov, passed through passport control with no trouble. His was a genuine passport. However, problems arose as the Arabs presented their forged passports to the immigration officer. He didn't see many Kyrgyzstan passports but he had just checked the Emir's passport and had recently seen Temier and Askari's passports. The first Arab's passport didn't look quite right. It had significant differences from the other Kyrgyz passports which had recently come his way. He asked Ahmed al-Shayei his date of birth. Alarm bells rang in his mind when the date Ahmed stated was different from the one in the passport. He called a security officer to conduct Ahmed to a secure room while keeping the passport. The same problem arose as he checked the passports of the other two Arabs. The Bishkek forger hadn't even bothered to make his forgeries out with the actual dates of birth of the three travellers. If these travellers had checked on that, they didn't seem bothered by the discrepancy. In any case, they hadn't bothered to memorise the false information. The three Arabs were all taken to separate secure rooms and the immigration officer sent the passports to his senior officer to be checked. Yes, they were indeed forgeries.

They were now subject to interrogation in the separate rooms by the immigration authorities. The questions soon revealed that they weren't bona fide travellers. Ahmed al-Shayei claimed that the purpose of his visit was sightseeing but was unable to identify which particular sights he had come to see or why Diyarbakir could offer anything more special than what he had seen in Samarkand. Ahmed claimed he had also been sightseeing in Samarkand but couldn't recollect which particular sights he had found impressive. Kamal al Akaba stated that he had come on a shopping trip for clothes but couldn't explain what was so special about clothes in Diyarbakir which was different from those he could buy in Uzbekistan? Qutaiba Attougui simply claimed he was there because he was accompanying his boss who had some unspecified business in Diyarbakir. This immediately drew the immigration officer's attention to the fact that this Arab and almost certainly his two colleagues had an important connection with the Kyrgyz who had just passed unchallenged through immigration control.

Meanwhile, the Emir, waiting for the Arabs in the baggage collection area by the conveyor, was getting increasingly impatient. He returned to the passport checking area to find out what was the cause of the delay but wasn't allowed back. The officer on duty at the exit to passport control asked to see the Emir's passport. It looked in order. He handed it back and simply told the Emir that there was an irregularity with the passports of those about whom he was enquiring. This immediately rang alarm bells in the Emir's mind. He immediately left the airport and booked himself into a hotel in the city centre.

The three Arabs were detained overnight in separate cells while the immigration officers compared notes. They soon realized that there was no coherent reason for their being in Diyarbakir. Although travelling together, they all seemed to have different reasons for being there, none of which was open to further explanation. They contacted their counterparts in Kyrgyzstan and confirmed that no passports had been officially issued to individuals with these names. They discovered that it was believed that the three Arabs were wanted by the Uzbek police for an attack carried out in broad daylight in Tashkent.

The immigration authorities came to the conclusion that these three were up to no good and should be further detained. This conclusion was reinforced when a customs search of their baggage revealed murderous looking knives concealed, both from normal sight and the perception of X-rays, by a false steel panel in the base of their cases. It seemed quite possible that they were members of Isil, returning to the area to create more trouble. The Kurds had distressing memories of Isil. The PKK (Kurdistan Workers' Party) had fought bitter battles with Isil and had no love for them. They had first-hand awareness of atrocities carried out by Isil. These men they had detained had names characteristic of Isil fighters. From interviews with Isil prisoners, records had been derived of names of their fellow fighters who hadn't been captured. The authorities would arrange to trawl through these names to discover if the three Arabs, now in Kurdish custody, were included.

The name of the fourth member of the party who had not been detained was Natalya Almazbekov. He had been described by one of the Arabs as the boss. He may not have been involved in the fighting but they concluded that he had probably contributed to Isil finances from outside the region. If they were correct in their conclusion, this would make him every bit as guilty in their eyes as those who carried out the fighting. This conclusion was reinforced when further questioning of the Arab detainees indicated that the reason they carried little money on their persons was that they were financed by Natalya Almazbekov whom they always referred to as the Emir.

The Kurdish investigation revealed that the three Arabs were indeed former Isil fighters. Having made this connection, they were immediately thrown into the prison reserved for Isil combatants. Conditions here were not good. Further investigations would be carried out to discover whether or not they had had any direct involvement in the atrocities which had been committed during this war.

Meanwhile, the Emir had booked into a hotel and spent a sleepless night, wondering what was happening to his three Arab religious policemen and what they were saying to the Kurdish immigration authorities. The following morning, he came down to breakfast and settled at a table near the window from which he could both look outside, observe his fellow guests and see what was going on in the reception hall. His attention was drawn to the headlines in Arabic in the newspaper being read by the hotel guest on the next table.

Three suspected Isil terrorists detained at Diyarbakir airport.

The police are searching for a fourth member of the party believed to be a Moslem cleric.

The Emir's anxiety was heightened when he saw a police car pull up outside the hotel. Three armed police left the car and entered the hotel lobby. The Emir didn't wait to be arrested. He immediately got up, followed a waiter through the service door and found himself in the hotel kitchen from whence he could see a door opening into the yard. Once in the yard he began to gather his thoughts. He realised that if the police were hot in pursuit, someone of his age had no chance of outrunning them. He looked around the yard. There were some large waste bins. He opened the first one. It was full of leftover food. The second one was filled with black plastic bags containing rubbish. This looked cleaner than the waste food bin. He climbed inside, lowered the lid and waited. It was dark. The only sound was the Emir's rapidly beating heart. In the darkness, the Emir couldn't accurately estimate the passage of time. After a few minutes, he could hear voices in the yard. He held his breath. Then the voices receded. No-one had looked inside the bins. Over the next ten minutes or quarter of an hour, nothing more could be heard. The Emir continued to remain in hiding for sometime longer. After what must have been at least half an hour, he cautiously opened the lid and peered out. There was nobody around. He climbed out.

What was he to do next? All his belongings were in his room. He dared not go back past the reception desk. He went back into the kitchen which he had run through some time earlier in making his escape. He attracted puzzled stares from the cooks and kitchen staff. He found another door out of the kitchen and discovered the back stairs. He climbed these and returned to his room without meeting anybody else. He packed his case. He froze as he looked through the window and saw a police car draw up. The kitchen staff had informed reception that the Emir had returned into the hotel. A few minutes later, someone tried his room door. Where could he hide? The wardrobe and the en-suite were too obvious. He grabbed the bed cover, picked up his case and stepped on to the balcony. He crouched down on the corner of the balcony which was out of direct site from the room and covered himself with the bed cover.

He heard his room door being unlocked from the outside and people talking, but he could not understand what was being said. Whoever had come into the room soon left after a cursory look round. They didn't check the balcony. The Emir remained where he was. A few minutes later the room maid came in to service the room. Where was the bed cover? Then she noticed that a corner of the bed cover was showing just outside the balcony. She went out to retrieve it. She pulled it off the Emir, gave a piercing scream when she saw this old man huddled there and ran back into the room. The Emir sprang to his feet and chased the chamber maid into the room, grabbed her and tried to place his hand across her mouth to stem this hysterical screaming. However, the alarm had already been heard. Nearby hotel staff rushed to the room and pulled the Emir off the maid. They were followed by the police who were still in the building and had heard the scream.

"We're taking you into custody," said the senior police officer speaking in a language the Emir could understand.

"You can't do that," objected the Emir. "I haven't committed any crime."

"Well, assaulting a female member of the hotel staff will do for starters," replied the police officer, "and from what we've heard from your colleagues, I think that there will be more charges to follow."

With that, the Emir was handcuffed and taken down to the police station where further investigations would be carried out into his involvement with Isil, even if this was not direct involvement in the fighting but funding the organisation from a distance. We don't know if any war crimes or violation of human rights charges came to light to be levelled at the three Arabs but involvement with Isil was a sufficient crime to ensure that all four of them would spend a considerable time in a Kurdish jail where conditions were far from good.

The news of the Emir's arrest was fed back to the Kyrgyz press and hence discovered by the inhabitants of Nann Kol. Soon after that, Temier and Askari received an e-mail from their friends which completely allayed their fears about returning home. They had read in one of the Kyrgyz newspapers of the arrest in Diyarbakir of four people from Kyrgyzstan on charges of attempted illegal entry into Turkey with a view to carrying out terrorist offences and that they had been confined to a Kurdish prison for an indefinite period. The four were obviously the Emir and has Arab associates. The report had appeared in English newspapers but in small print in the middle pages and had been missed by our friends. The way was now clear for a safe return to Kyrgyzstan.

On the day of departure, the six friends travelled to Birmingham airport to say their farewells. As there were no direct flights from the United Kingdom to Kyrgyzstan, they would travel home by following the route that Jason and Becky had used on their outward journey and fly via Istanbul. They had all had such a wonderful and adventurous time together that it was hard to say goodbye. The parting was quite emotional. However, they all vowed to meet up again in the hopefully not too distant future.

A few days later, Becky received an email thanking her, her parents and her friends for the absolutely lovely time Temier and Askari had spent in England and letting her know that everything was as well ordered as they could have hoped for when they returned home. Indeed, it was better than hoped for. The Kyrgyz authorities had become aware of irregularities in the way the religious police had carried out their duties in Nann Kol and the town was now patrolled by the regular Kyrgyz police force.

There was no further role for the Islamic religious police.

Becky and Jason, Bill and Liz were overjoyed to hear this reassuring news. The time spent in Transoxiana was a recurrent theme of conversations between the four of them as they revelled in the nostalgia conjured up by recalling that wonderful and adventurous time spent in Transoxiana.

The books published by Midhurst have been written by Dr Ray Filby who has had many years' experience of church life in a number of churches, fulfilling at various times the roles of Pathfinder Group Leader, Youth Fellowship Leader, Secretary to the Parochial Church Council, Churchwarden and Reader (Licensed Lay Minister). This experience is reflected in the stories he writes which embrace several genres, including historical fiction, short stories, Bible study, murder stories and romantic fiction. They are all available from Amazon in paperback or Kindle form.

The Sun and the Moon of Alexandria

This is a fictional biopic of Apollos, a missionary saint and one of St. Paul's co-workers. Although mentioned many times in the New Testament, little is known of the life and background of Apollos. Thus, there is scope to create a story which constructs a feasible account of Apollos' youth in Egypt, his journey to Israel, his conversion, his relationship with St. Paul, his missionary work and his marriage. The story culminates in his martyrdom. In situations where Apollos interacts with well-known Biblical characters, the narrative remains faithful to the New Testament account.

(This book is published by the Book Guild)

Parables, the Greatest Stories ever told - Retold

'The Greatest Stories ever told – Retold' focuses on the better known parables of Jesus and rewrites them as situations in modern life which correspond to the situations in Jesus' day, attempting to promote the same teaching that Jesus was giving in the original parable. Each parable is preceded by a modern translation of the original parable and followed by ten questions which are suitable for a person's private devotions or for use in the context of a group Bible study.

St. Columba's— Its Life and Its People

Churches are living organisms, each with their own distinctive patterns of life. While their members experience the same ups and downs in life as the population as a whole, their Christian faith results in their reacting to circumstances in a distinctive way.

This book is a set of short stories, some of which trace the unfolding of events which occur as part of church life, and others which recount the experience of individual church members. Readers are invited to consider the practical or ethical problems which arise in these stories and think how they themselves might have dealt with or reacted to these situations.

The Countess who should have been Queen

Margaret Plantagenet was born near the end of the Wars of the Roses. As the daughter of the brother of King Edward IV, a situation could well have arisen when she or her brother, Edward, had a claim to the throne. Margaret was not ambitious to become Queen but was happy to marry a commoner and settled as an enlightened landowner with her husband in Berkshire. Margaret became Queen Catherine of Aragon's chief lady-in-waiting and was awarded a peerage to become Countess of Salisbury. Margaret faithfully supported Catherine right through her reign and as far as she could when Catherine was sent to live in isolation after her divorce. One of Margaret's sons, Reginald, became a prominent churchman and angered the King by writing a treatise, heavily critical of Henry VIII, the way he had divorced Catherine and taken over the Church of England. Reginald was living out of reach of Henry on the continent so Henry vented his wrath on Margaret and her family.

Consequences of Immature Love

Boy-Girl, Man-Woman relationships cement our society. Because these relationships are seldom straightforward, they provide scope for an indefinite number of works of fiction. In this novel, you are invited to follow the amorous adventures of Georgina Matthews and Arthur Gray from the time they leave school and start at university until they ultimately marry the partner for whom they seemed destined from the outset.

The story told might be of special interest to a young person embarking on the minefield of love and courtship as they consider the factors which led to the success or failure of the relationships encountered in this novel. Ethical factors are involved and it is significant that a shared Christian faith led to the final happy outcome.

Soldiers, Saints and Sinners

'*Soldiers, Saints and Sinners*' is a collection of fictitious stories, featuring some of the minor characters whom Jesus encountered in his ministry. It attempts to suggest how their backgrounds might have been important in the way they led to their encounter with Jesus and the way these encounters furthered the progress of Jesus' ministry. Each story is preceded by a modern Biblical translation of the passage which recounts their appearance on the scene where Jesus was ministering and is followed by five questions which are suitable for a person's private devotions or for use in the context of a group Bible study.

The Tasks of Chronavon

When sensible twelve-year-olds, Alfred and Alice meet a mysterious angel called Chronavon in the vestry of their church, it seems someone is playing a practical joke on them. After all, angels don't just pop up in church vestries to enlist the help of two young people to journey back in time to prevent a devilish time traveller from altering the course of history. Yet it soon becomes clear that Chronavon's incredible story is true. As Alfred and Alice are whisked backwards through the centuries, they become immersed in the rich customs and costumes of the past through Henry III's troubled reign, the insecurity of Princess Elizabeth before she became Queen Elizabeth I and the Civil War between the Cavaliers and Roundheads. 'The Tasks of Chronavon' is an exciting, informative tale for young readers which effortlessly weaves fact and fiction with a sprinkling of humour and shows how little human values have changed over time.

The Evil Occupants of Easingdale Castle

Teenager, Jason, and his friends, Bill, Becky and Liz, are recruited by an unusual messenger to pit their wits against an international gang of forgers, occupying their local castle. The gang are intent on destabilising the British economy by flooding the country with forged £20 notes which could pass off as the real thing. The gang is well equipped with hi-tech machines.

It remains to be seen whether Jason and his friends, who are also technically knowledgeable, can outwit the gang.

 Technology will have advanced since this book was written and young readers are invited to consider whether they could have done better than Jason and his friends with equipment now available.

A Church like Cluedo

After graduating from college as a civil engineer, Annette Owen had hoped to work in the developing world under the auspices of a missionary society. When this door to Christian service was closed, she applied to become an ordained minister but was turned down by the selection committee. She was however able to exercise a very fulfilled ministry as a clergy wife. Unfortunately, her clergy husband had dark secrets in his life of which Annette was totally unaware until a situation arose which resulted in murder being committed. The impact of this had an unexpected effect on the course of Annette's life.

Inspector Sinclair and Sergeant Powers' most interesting cases

This account of some interesting cases solved by the detective duo, Inspector Sinclair and Sergeant Powers, is not a normal 'whodunnit' in which the murderer is not revealed until the very end when the detective reveals the clues which he or she alone has picked up to solve the case without sharing their significance with the reader until the very end.

The stories in this book are divided into sections, a list of those involved to help the reader keep track of the characters,

'the Event' which describes the situation when the murder took place,

'the Investigation' which describes the systematic way in which the detectives investigated the case and

'the Evidence' in which the crucial evidence by which a cast iron case against the murderer was built up, is reviewed.

An Insight into the Gospels and the Book of Acts

'An Insight into the Gospels and the Book of Acts' is an overview of the themes, contents, emphases, and structure of the first five books of the New Testament. While there is so much similarity in the stories and teaching in each of the gospels, this book contrasts the way each gospel is written and presented. It highlights the quite remarkable differences which exist between each of the gospels as they are directed to different audiences and have different primary objectives. The book is presented with the main content of the book appearing on the right hand (odd numbered) pages and supportive texts placed opposite the relevant passages on the left hand pages.

Puzzles, Quiz and Activities Suitable for Social Events

Volumes 1, 2, 3 & 4

These books consist of a set of puzzles, quiz and activities which the author designed for use at a monthly social event organised by St. Michael's, Church, Budbrooke, in the Community Centre in the part of the parish known as Chase Meadow. People who have opted to take part really seem to have enjoyed these activities which are interesting rather than extremely challenging. While a good general knowledge is helpful in completing some of the activities, they are not designed to expose people's ignorance as data sheets and appropriate reference books like atlases are made available to help participants find any information needed. Thus, the activities are educational.

The socials run at Chase Meadow are not restricted to church members but all and sundry are invited as part of the church outreach. With many of the activities, a final stage often involves deciphering a phrase, quote or saying. As the socials are sponsored by the church, many of the quotes to be deciphered are Biblical texts. However, anyone choosing to use these ideas could quite easily modify the final stage and use a secular quote rather than a Biblical text to be deciphered.

143